OFF THE LEASH

Daring Dachshund Mystery, Book 1

By Cynthia Hickey

Chapter One

"**Here we are,** Minnie girl." I smiled down at my long-haired, black and brown, miniature Dachshund, then inserted the key into apartment number one. The apartment reserved for the manager.

The last thing I expected after my aunt, Mary Jane, fell down the stairs of Riverside Towers, breaking her neck, was to inherit the two hundred apartments. What did I know about managing an apartment complex? I, Crystal Waters, had never been out of the small town of Walnut Hills in all my twenty-eight years. I'd spent those years working as an administrative assistant at Riverside Elementary, filing paperwork and answering phones. Nothing in my experience prepared me for landlord duties.

I pushed open the door and stepped into a cluttered, doily-filled living room. Yikes. It would take me a year of Sundays to clear out the things that my aunt left me. Her decorating style was definitely not the minimalistic style I preferred.

Minnie sniffed cautiously at the doorframe before venturing inside, her nails clicking on the hardwood floor. The scent of lavender and dust filled my nostrils, bringing back memories of childhood visits when Aunt Mary Jane would serve tea in delicate china cups and lecture me about posture.

Leaving Minnie to get acquainted with her new home, I wandered the two-bedroom apartment. Each room was worse than the first. Porcelain dolls, stuffed animals, Victorian figurines…every surface contained so many collectables you couldn't see the wood underneath. A brass clock ticked loudly from the mantel, flanked by ceramic cats with unsettling glass eyes. Lace doilies covered every flat surface, yellowed with age.

I sneezed, threw open the master bedroom curtains, and looked down on a nicely landscaped courtyard with tables and grilles circling a sparkling swimming pool. At least the view was pleasant. The afternoon sun glinted off the water, and a few residents lounged in chairs, reading or chatting. This place had potential, if I could just figure out how to run it.

The bedroom itself was a shrine to floral patterns. The bedspread, curtains, and wallpaper all competed in a riot of roses, daisies, and lilies. I made a mental note to start the decluttering process in here first. I needed somewhere to sleep that didn't make me feel like a garden had swallowed me.

I headed for the second bedroom. An L-shaped desk filled one corner, and a fold-out sofa bed on the opposite wall. A small filing cabinet stood under one section of the desk. This room was surprisingly uncluttered. The walls were painted a soft sage green, and a single landscape painting hung above the sofa. This could be my office.

I sat at the desk and opened the laptop. To my right rested a bright pink folder. On the front, in my aunt's neat cursive handwriting, were the words "Tenants, problems, and other details." I smiled and opened the folder. I didn't read far before I frowned.

A few of the tenants didn't seem to care for Aunt Mary Jane. At least not according to her notes. A Mr. Hank Miller, apartment #2, complained often that Mary Jane was too nosy for her own good and never kept up with repairs. He actually told my aunt to watch her step. The note was dated three weeks before her fall. My stomach tightened at the coincidence.

The tenant in apartment 125, a Ms. Linda Hooper, professional dog walker, didn't seem to care for the fact that my aunt was constantly on her to clean up after the dogs she walked. Told the woman to head to the nearby dog park rather than use the courtyard. The big thing written next to the woman's name was that she blamed my aunt for turning a blind eye to the death of a dog in Linda's care. Aunt Mary Jane had underlined the words "false accusation" three times.

Nothing major, other than the dog's death, but

something about the meticulous note-taking on residents who didn't get along with my aunt left a bad taste in my mouth. As for the others, no mention except for repairs needed and completed. Leaky faucet in 203. Broken dishwasher in 156. Screen door replacement in 89.

The fact that I would be required to fix toilets and broken appliances scared me spitless. I could barely change a lightbulb without standing on a chair and second-guessing myself. Maybe I should consider selling Riverside Towers. I'd quit my job as an administration assistant at an elementary school, but the apartment complex should sell for enough to give me a sizeable nest egg. The one thing that kept me from listing the place was that my aunt's lawyer said my aunt stipulated in her will that I keep the place for at least a year. After that, I was free to do whatever I wanted.

One year. Twelve months of dealing with tenant complaints and maintenance issues. Could I survive that long?

"So, we make do, right, Minnie?" I glanced at my waiting pup, who sat near my feet with her ears perked forward. "How about a visit to the dog park? Get us both out of this stuffy apartment?"

Her tail thumped against the floor, and she let out an excited yip.

"Good. Settling in and boxing up can wait." I snatched her leash from where I'd dropped it on the coffee table, led her outside, and locked the door behind me.

The autumn afternoon air was crisp and pleasant, carrying the scent of freshly cut grass. I took a deep breath, letting the tension ease from my shoulders. The walk would do us both good.

The dog park wasn't hard to find. I followed a young woman with five dogs on leashes, all different breeds and sizes, moving in a surprisingly coordinated pack. She must be a professional walker, I thought, watching how effortlessly she managed them all.

The dog park was situated near a small, man-made pond, although the sign said lake. In my mind, it wasn't large enough to qualify as a lake. Ducks paddled near the far shore, and a weeping willow dipped its branches into the water. A paved path circled the entire area, dotted with benches and trash receptacles.

Minnie growled and made noises in her throat all the way around the lake and into the fenced section for small dogs. Right next to it was another for larger dogs. The small dog area had about six other dogs running and playing, their owners chatting in small clusters. After spending a few minutes making sure none of the other pets were aggressive, I removed Minnie's leash. She promptly leaned against me and shivered.

"Don't be scared, sweetie. Go play." I crouched down and stroked her silky ears.

I got a mournful whine in response. A Yorkie trotted over to investigate, and Minnie buried her face against my leg and snarled.

"You're new here." The woman I'd followed sat down next to me on a weathered wooden bench.

"Yes. I'm Crystal Waters. The new manager and owner of Riverside Towers." I smiled, settling onto the bench beside her.

Her eyes widened. "Really? I'm Linda Hooper. I'm in apartment two-hundred." Her gaze fell on Minnie. "Aren't you a beauty? What's her name?"

"Minnie." My smile widened as it always did when someone complimented my fur baby. "I love her so much, I want to get another."

"I can recommend a good breeder when you're ready." Linda stared at the other pet owners, her expression shifting to something more calculating. "That hunk of man flesh with the German Shepherd in the next pen is Lance Hendricks. He lives at Riverside, too, in number 117. He stays to himself, unfortunately." She sighed dramatically. "Believe me, I've tried getting his attention."

My gaze followed hers to a tall, dark-haired man throwing a ball for a gorgeous German Shepherd to fetch. The dog moved with fluid grace, powerful and obedient. Lance himself had an athletic build and moved with a slight limp that somehow didn't diminish his presence. "Any other residents here?"

"No." She shook her head, her ponytail swinging. "But that man in the business suit who looks out of place is Richard Thornton, a wealthy developer. He wants to buy this entire park for a luxury condo project.

So far, petitions from the residents of Riverside have kept him from doing so." She cut me a side look. "I've heard that he's also after Riverside Towers."

"Really?" I didn't see anything in my aunt's notes. My aunt had been thorough about documenting tenant conflicts, but nothing about outside threats to the property.

"Hmm hmm. No one likes him. Rumor is that he swindled a man named Mark Shuford out of a lot of money. Then, there's Jack Bradley, who is all about the environment. Thornton and his daughter, Victoria, keep the gossip columns running with their weekly attacks on each other over a woman named Emma…something. Oh." She motioned her head toward a middle-aged man standing near the pond with a tablet in his hands. "That's David Reeves. He works for Thornton. Probably measuring up the place for demolition."

I studied Richard Thornton more closely. He stood rigidly in his expensive suit, looking completely out of place among the casual dog owners in jeans and T-shirts. His silver hair was perfectly styled, and he checked his phone every few seconds with sharp, impatient movements.

"What do you think about Thornton?"

Her smile faded, and she stiffened. "Can't stand the sight of the man. He left his prescription medication on the bench right where you're sitting, and a dog I was taking care of got into them and died." Her voice dropped. "A sweet little Pomeranian named Buttercup.

The owner was devastated. Sued me, even though it wasn't my fault. Your aunt refused to back me up, said I should have been more careful."

I felt a pang of sympathy despite my aunt's notes painting a different picture. "I'm so sorry. That must have been awful."

"Oh, look. Lance is leaving the dog park. Don't look."

Of course, I looked. I stood as his dark gaze met mine, those intense brown eyes locking onto my face. My foot hooked on the leg of the bench, and I toppled backward to roll down the hill with Minnie barking as she gave chase. My world became a blur of grass and sky, dignity completely abandoned.

Linda burst into laughter as I lay there and stared at the sky above, trying to catch my breath.

Minnie licked my face, her warm tongue swiping across my nose.

Seconds after I rolled, Lance stared down at me and offered a hand to help me up. "Are you okay?" Concern creased his forehead.

I nodded and accepted his help, his hand warm and strong around mine. "Just clumsy."

"She's the new owner of the Towers," Linda said, still giggling.

Face heated, I glared at her, then bent to pick up Minnie, who wriggled in my arms. "Thank you, Lance."

"How do you know my...oh. The local rumor

mill." He glanced at Linda. "I suppose she's been filling you in on everyone and everything."

"Pretty much."

"Don't believe everything she says." He gave me a nod, then limped away, his German Shepherd walking obediently at his side.

"Isn't he the most handsome man you've ever met?" Linda pretended to swoon, fanning herself with one hand.

"He is nice on the eyes." I clicked Minnie's leash on her halter, ready to escape before I embarrassed myself further. "See you around."

After I exited the pen, then pulled the gate shut, I whirled to find my nose smashed against a T-shirt-covered chest. I gasped and stepped back, stopping when my back met the fence. My gaze lifted to see Lance. "Sorry."

"No worries. My dog, King, seems interested in your little one."

Sure enough, Minnie met the Shepherd nose-to-nose, her tail wagging. "She hates other dogs."

"Not mine." A faint smile graced his lips, transforming his serious expression into something softer. "You headed back to the Towers?"

I nodded, not trusting my voice.

"I'll walk with you."

Mercy. I could barely form a coherent sentence around the man, and now he wanted to walk three blocks with me? So, I nodded and fell into step beside him.

We didn't speak for the first block. I was acutely aware of his presence beside me, the way King and Minnie seemed perfectly content to walk together. Finally, I found my voice. "You knew my aunt?"

"Yes. Mary Jane was a good woman. I was sorry to hear about her accident."

"Did you…did you notice anything unusual before she fell?"

He gave me a sharp look. "Why do you ask?"

"Just curious. I found some notes she kept about tenants who had problems with her."

"Mary Jane kept notes on everything." His expression was unreadable. "She was thorough, sometimes to a fault."

We didn't speak again until we stopped at the door to my apartment. "I helped your aunt with the handy work around here," Lance said. "Let me know if I can do the same for you." He turned and headed across the courtyard, leaving me with my mouth hanging open.

Once I got control of myself again, I stepped back into my home and leaned against the door. What a strange day. A handsome man I'd just met offered me his services, and a woman my aunt believed didn't like her had filled me in on every Riverside citizen in sight.

Minnie looked up at me and whined.

"I know, girl. This is going to be an interesting year."

Chapter Two

My shoulders slumped as I plopped into my aunt's—my—office chair and scanned the list of residents' concerns. Some were easy. Apartment 106 just needed a new battery in its smoke detector, but 111 had a stuffed toilet that had overflowed and spilled into the hallway. Below that, someone in 203 complained about a leaky faucet that dripped all night, keeping them awake. Apartment 89 had submitted three separate requests about a broken garbage disposal.

I rubbed my temples. This was only day two, and already I felt overwhelmed. The pink folder sat to my right, Aunt Mary Jane's neat handwriting a reminder that she'd managed this place for fifteen years without complaint. If she could do it, so could I.

I slipped my cell phone into my pocket, grabbed a mop, bucket, and a small toolbox I found in the closet, then headed to 111. The hallway smelled faintly of air freshener, probably someone's attempt to mask the odor wafting from under the door. After several knocks, a man answered.

"About time." He scowled and stepped back so I could enter.

The smell hit me first, then the water pooling in the hallway. This would not be the highlight of my day. My stomach churned as I took in the soggy carpet and water-stained baseboards. "How did this happen?"

"I knocked my deodorant in the toilet."

"And you didn't fish it out?" I narrowed my eyes.

"That's disgusting and not my job. That's why you get paid the big bucks. I've got to go to work. Mop is in the closet." He whirled and marched from the apartment, leaving the door wide open behind him.

Wow. Just wow. I stood there for a moment, staring at the mess, wondering if property management was really worth whatever rent income I'd be collecting. I dug a paper mask from my aunt's supplies, donned elbow-length latex gloves and removed the stick of deodorant from the toilet, then flushed. Idiot. Everything worked fine. The water swirled down without issue, proving the entire disaster could have been avoided if he'd just reached in and grabbed the stupid thing.

After mopping up the water, wringing out the mop multiple times into the bucket, I left the mop and bucket in the tub for the man to deal with and headed to the next thing on my to-do list. My back already ached, and I'd only been at this for an hour.

An elderly woman in apartment 106 greeted me with a warm smile and fresh-baked cookies. "You're Mary Jane's niece? Oh, you poor dear. Come in, come in." She ushered me inside an apartment that smelled of cinnamon and vanilla. "That beeping is driving me absolutely batty."

"I'll have it fixed in just a minute, Mrs.—"

"Henderson. But please, call me Betty." She pressed a plate of still-warm chocolate chip cookies into my hands. "Your aunt was such a dear woman. Always so helpful."

I balanced the cookies while climbing a small stepladder to reach the smoke detector. "You knew her well?"

"Oh yes. We played bridge every Thursday evening. I still can't believe she's gone." Betty's voice trembled. "Such a terrible accident. She was always so careful on those stairs."

My hands paused on the smoke detector. "You don't think it was an accident?"

Betty wrung her hands. "I shouldn't speak ill, but there were people who weren't happy with her. That Mr. Miller in apartment two was always complaining. And that developer, Thornton, kept pestering her to sell. She told him no a dozen times, but he wouldn't take no for an answer."

I filed that information away and replaced the battery, the beeping finally stopping. "There you go, Betty. All fixed."

"You're an angel. Take the cookies, dear. You look like you could use them. You're far too skinny."

The next stop was apartment 134, where an older man needed the chain put back on the thingie in his toilet tank. I really needed to learn the proper terminology if I were to be doing these things for at least a year. Mr. Patterson showed me to the bathroom and explained how the chain had somehow come loose from the flapper.

"Not sure how it happened," he said, scratching his head. "One day it worked fine, next day it didn't."

I removed the tank lid, grateful this repair didn't involve actual sewage, and reattached the chain to the flapper mechanism. "Should be good now."

"Mary Jane would have figured it out in half the time." He chuckled at my expression. "No offense, dear. She'd been doing this for years. You'll get the hang of it."

I hoped he was right. After saying goodbye, I stepped back outside.

"Good morning."

I turned and smiled at the sight of Lance strolling my way, King trotting obediently beside him. "Good morning to you."

"Need any help?" His gaze fell to the tool bag in my hand.

Heat crept up my neck as I remembered my embarrassing tumble yesterday. At least he didn't mention it. "Know anything about washing machines?"

While all the apartments had washer and dryer hookups, some residents used the common laundry room. "I've been told one of them has stopped working."

"I've got a few minutes to take a look."

We walked together to the laundromat, a spacious area in the building's basement with ten washers and ten dryers lined up against opposite walls. The fluorescent lights flickered overhead, and the air held that distinctive combination of detergent and humidity. A woman was folding clothes at one of the long tables, barely glancing up at us.

When we reached the offending washer, he asked me what I knew, if anything, about appliances. I shrugged and gave the machine a good kick with my right foot. It shuddered and started. "Hey, it worked."

His eyes widened before a laugh escaped him, rich and warm. It transformed his usually serious face into one way too handsome. "Not exactly the method I would recommend." He turned off the washer and pulled it away from the wall with seemingly little effort. "Definitely needs a good cleaning. You could make a blanket out of the cobwebs and dust bunnies back here."

I hopped up to sit on another machine and watched him work, his movements efficient and confident. King lay down near the door, content to wait. "I think I need to take some classes."

"Classes?" He glanced over his shoulder.

"You know, basic home repair, appliance maintenance, plumbing. I'm completely out of my depth here." I swung my legs, feeling about twelve years old while admitting my inadequacy. "I can organize files and answer phones with the best of them, but ask me to fix a garbage disposal and I'm lost."

He wiped his hands on a rag, pulling out various tools from his own bag. "Most of this stuff is common sense and experience. You'll learn as you go."

"Or I could hire someone who actually knows what they're doing."

"You could." He examined the washer's drainage system. "But that would eat into your profits pretty quickly. Riverside has two hundred units. Even if only a fraction need repairs each month, the costs add up."

I hadn't thought of that. "Good point."

He worked in silence for a few minutes, tightening connections and clearing out lint buildup. I found myself studying his profile, the concentration on his face, the capable way he handled the tools. Finally, he straightened. "Give it a try now."

I hopped down and started the machine. It ran smoothly, no strange noises or vibrations. "You're a miracle worker."

"Hardly." He repacked his tools. "I'll make a deal with you. Give me my rent for free, and I'll fix anything you need me to around here."

After running some numbers through my head, I nodded and thrust out my hand. "You've got a deal.

Will it interfere with your work?"

"Nope." He returned the handshake, his grip firm and warm. "I'm on medical leave right now. When I do start back, I can help on evenings and weekends."

I wanted to ask why he was on leave, wanted to know what he did for a living, but held my tongue, instead focusing on the way his warm hand felt as it engulfed mine. The calluses on his palm suggested physical work. His handshake was confident without being aggressive. I'd been without a relationship for far too long. Not that I expected to be in one with Lance, silly me. We were simply two people helping each other.

"With you doing the hard stuff, I can do the easy things like replacing batteries and lightbulbs." I hopped from the washing machine, breaking the handshake that had lasted a beat too long. "If you have this under control, I've got to let my Minnie out. Catch up to you later?"

"Absolutely." He returned his attention to the machine, checking his repairs one more time. "Oh, and you should have my email on my lease. Just forward me any repairs that are needed, and I'll take care of them. You won't have to worry about a thing."

"Thanks. Love you!" I stiffened, my entire body going rigid. "Oh, uh…" I darted from the room, my face flaming. I hadn't meant that in any but the friendliest way. It was something I said to my girlfriends all the time, a casual sign-off. But saying it to Lance, a man I barely knew, a man who made my pulse race?

Outside, I leaned against the nearest wall and buried my face in my hands. As my heart rate returned to normal, I lifted my head and rushed back to my apartment. I splashed cold water on my face, then clicked Minnie's leash to her halter. "Girl, your owner is a real piece of work."

The look on her face let me know she agreed. Her ears drooped, and she tilted her head as if to say, "What did you do now?"

"Let's skip the dog park today and take the walking path around the lake." I was in no hurry to return to the apartment complex and see Lance, and the path would take longer than some time at the dog park. I didn't think I could ever face him again. Maybe I could send him repair requests exclusively by email for the next year. That seemed reasonable.

The path winding through the trees around the five-acre lake felt cooler. Dappled sunlight filtered through the canopy of oak and maple trees, their leaves rustling in the gentle breeze. I let Minnie stretch her leash as far as it would go. Nose to the ground, she swerved from one side of the path to the other, stopping only long enough to bark at a squirrel chattering at us from a tree branch.

A jogger passed us going the opposite direction, earbuds in, barely acknowledging our presence. An older couple sat on one of the benches overlooking the water, feeding ducks that paddled hopefully nearby. The normalcy of it all helped settle my nerves.

As we walked, the grossness of toilet cleaning and the embarrassment of talking to Lance like I did with my girlfriends fell from my shoulders. Peace settled over me like a soft blanket, and I let Minnie off her leash. The lake sparkled in the afternoon sun, and birds sang from the trees. This was nice. Maybe I could make this work. Maybe managing Riverside Towers wouldn't be so terrible if I had Lance's help and places like this to escape to.

It took me a minute to realize I had now gotten ahead of Minnie and that my dog refused to leave a certain bush. "Come on, girl. I'm sure lots of dogs have relieved themselves there." I gave her halter a tug to no avail.

She planted her feet, her entire body rigid, and let out a low growl. That wasn't like her. Minnie was timid, not aggressive, unless you were a dog invading her space.

Sighing, I moved toward her, parted the bush, and gasped. I stumbled back and landed hard on my rearend, pain shooting up my tailbone.

Richard Thornton's lifeless eyes stared over at me. A bloodied rock lay near his head, dark stains spreading across the grass beneath him. His expensive suit was torn, and dirt smudged across his face. Fluttering from one of the thin branches was a torn piece of expensive fabric, caught as if he'd grabbed for it during a struggle.

My vision tunneled. My breath came in short, sharp gasps. This couldn't be happening. Not on my second day as property manager. The disgusting job of unplugging the toilet slid to number two on my awful things list.

Minnie whined and pressed against my leg.

With shaking hands, I pulled my cell phone out of my pocket and dialed 911. My fingers trembled so badly I almost dropped the phone.

"911, what's your emergency?"

"I...I found a body." My voice came out high and thin. "By the lake. The walking path. He's dead."

"Ma'am, can you confirm the person is deceased?"

I forced myself to look again at Richard Thornton's unseeing eyes, the unnatural angle of his head, the pool of blood. "Yes. He's definitely dead."

"Help is on the way. Stay on the line with me. Are you in a safe location?"

I glanced around the peaceful path. The trees suddenly seemed menacing rather than comforting. Was the killer still nearby? Had they been watching when I discovered the body? "I...I think so."

"What's your name, ma'am?"

"Crystal Waters."

In the distance, I heard the wail of sirens growing closer.

Chapter Three

The sirens grew louder, then stopped abruptly. Car doors slammed, voices shouted orders, and the heavy tread of boots pounded on the paved path. The 911 operator continued talking, her voice steady and calming, but I couldn't focus on her words. All I could see was Richard Thornton's face, pale and lifeless.

"Crystal?"

I jerked my head up to see Lance jogging down the path, King at his side. His face was tight with concern, his dark eyes scanning the area with an intensity that seemed almost professional.

"I'm here with someone," I told the operator, my voice shaking. "A friend."

"That's good. The officers are almost at your location. You can disconnect when they arrive."

Lance dropped to one knee beside me, his hand automatically reaching out to steady me. "What happened? I heard the sirens from my apartment and knew you had come this way." His gaze shifted to the bushes, and his entire demeanor changed. His jaw tightened, and something flickered across his face—recognition, maybe, or professional assessment.

"I found him. Thornton. He's..." I couldn't finish the sentence.

"Stay here." Lance moved toward the body, careful not to disturb anything. He didn't touch Thornton, just observed from a respectful distance, his eyes cataloging details. When he returned, his expression was grim. "The police will want to talk to you. Just tell them exactly what happened."

"Miss Waters?" A tall Hispanic man in a charcoal suit approached, his badge clipped to his belt. Two uniformed officers flanked him, already securing the area with yellow crime scene tape. "I'm Detective Jon Martinez. I understand you discovered the body?"

I nodded, my throat too tight to speak.

Martinez pulled out a small notebook, his movements methodical and practiced. He was probably in his early forties, with salt-and-pepper hair cut short and observant brown eyes that missed nothing. "And you are?" He directed the question to Lance.

"Lance Hendricks. I live at Riverside Towers, apartment 117. I heard the commotion and came to check on Ms. Waters."

Something passed between the two men—a look of recognition or respect, I couldn't tell which.

Martinez's eyebrows rose slightly. "Hendricks? I thought you were on leave."

"I am." Lance's tone was clipped, professional.

"You two know each other?" I looked between them, confused.

"We've crossed paths." Martinez returned his attention to me, his expression softening. "Ms. Waters, I know this is difficult, but I need you to walk me through what happened. Start from the beginning."

I took a shaky breath, my hands trembling in my lap. Lance settled onto the ground beside me, close enough that I could feel the solid warmth of his presence. It helped, somehow, knowing he was there.

"I was walking my dog, Minnie." I glanced down at my Dachshund, who pressed against my leg, her leash again clipped to her halter. "We took the path around the lake. I wanted to clear my head after...after a stressful morning." Heat crept up my neck at the memory of my embarrassing slip earlier, but I pushed it aside. "Minnie stopped at that bush and wouldn't move. She was growling, which isn't like her. So, I went to see what was wrong, and I found..." My voice cracked.

"Take your time," Martinez said gently.

Lance's hand covered mine, warm and steady. The trembling in my fingers eased slightly. "I saw Mr. Thornton. The rock. The blood. I called 911 immediately."

"Did you touch anything? Move anything?"

"No. I fell backward when I saw him, but I didn't

touch the body or the scene." I swallowed hard. "Is he really...?"

"I'm afraid so." Martinez made notes in his book. "When did you start your walk?"

"Around two o'clock, maybe? I left my apartment at Riverside Towers and came straight here."

"Did you see anyone else on the path? Anyone leaving the area?"

I thought back, trying to remember through the fog of shock. "A jogger passed me going the other direction. And there was an older couple on a bench feeding ducks. They were near the far side of the lake."

Martinez nodded, writing quickly. "Can you describe them?"

"The jogger was a woman, I think. She had earbuds in and didn't really look at me. The couple..." I closed my eyes, trying to picture them. "The man was bald, wearing a blue windbreaker. The woman had white hair pulled back in a bun. That's all I remember."

"That's helpful, thank you." Martinez glanced at Lance. "You didn't see anything when you arrived?"

"No. I came from Riverside Towers when I heard the sirens. The path was empty except for Crystal." Lance's thumb brushed across my knuckles, a small gesture that I wasn't sure he was even aware of making.

A crime scene investigator approached, a woman in her thirties with red hair pulled back in a ponytail. "Detective? We've got the preliminary."

Martinez excused himself and walked a few feet

away, speaking in low tones with the investigator. I caught fragments of their conversation—"blunt force trauma," "between nine PM and midnight," "no identification on the body."

Lance leaned closer, his voice quiet. "How well did you know Thornton?"

"I didn't. Not really." I kept my voice equally low. "I saw him at the dog park yesterday. Linda Hooper pointed him out and said he wanted to buy the park for a development project. She also mentioned he'd been trying to buy Riverside Towers from my aunt."

Lance's expression sharpened. "Did your aunt ever mention him to you?"

"No, but I only found out about the inheritance a few days ago. We weren't close." Guilt twisted in my stomach. "I should have visited more often. Maybe if I had, she would have told me about problems with Thornton or other tenants."

"This isn't your fault." Lance's hand tightened on mine.

Martinez returned, his notebook open. "Ms. Waters, I need to ask you about your relationship with the deceased. Had you ever met Richard Thornton before yesterday?"

"No, never. Yesterday was the first time I saw him."

"And what were the circumstances?"

"I was at the dog park with Minnie. Linda Hooper, one of my tenants, was there and pointed him out. She told me he was a developer who wanted to buy the park." I hesitated. "She also said he'd been pressuring my aunt to sell Riverside Towers."

Martinez's pen scratched across the paper. "Your aunt being Mary Jane Waters?"

"Yes. She passed away a week ago. I inherited the property."

"I'm sorry for your loss." Martinez's expression remained neutral, but his eyes were sharp. "How did your aunt die?"

"She fell down the stairs at Riverside Towers. Broke her neck." The words came out flat, emotionless. I'd cried myself dry over Aunt Mary Jane already.

"Was there an investigation into her death?"

My stomach dropped. "I...I don't know. I assumed it was an accident. Should there have been?"

"Just routine questions." Martinez flipped to a new page. "Mr. Hendricks, where were you last night between nine PM and midnight?"

Lance didn't seem surprised by the question. "In my apartment. I was alone."

"Can anyone verify that?"

"No."

I stared at Lance, suddenly aware of how little I actually knew about him. He lived alone, was on medical leave from...what? He and Martinez clearly knew each other, which suggested law enforcement. But he hadn't mentioned any of that when we'd talked.

Martinez turned back to me. "And you, Ms.

Waters?"

"I was in my apartment too. Alone except for Minnie." I frowned. "You don't think I had anything to do with this?"

"I'm just establishing timelines." Martinez's tone remained professional. "This is standard procedure in any homicide investigation."

Homicide. The word hung in the air like a weight.

"Ms. Waters had no motive to harm Thornton," Lance said, his voice taking on an edge. "She didn't even know the man."

"Unless he was pressuring her to sell her property the same way he pressured her aunt." Martinez met Lance's gaze steadily. "I'm not accusing anyone. I'm gathering information."

Lance subsided, but tension radiated from him.

"Can you think of anyone who might have wanted to harm Mr. Thornton?" Martinez asked me.

I thought about Linda's comments at the dog park. "Linda Hooper blamed him for a dog's death. She said he left prescription medication on a bench, and the dog got into it. She seemed pretty angry about it."

"Anyone else?"

"There was another man Linda mentioned—Mark Shuford. She said Thornton swindled him out of money. And someone named Jack Bradley, who had environmental concerns about Thornton's development plans." I paused, remembering. "Oh, and Thornton's daughter, Victoria. Linda said they kept getting into public arguments about a woman."

Martinez wrote it all down. "You're very observant."

"Linda's very talkative," I corrected. "I was just trying to get to know my neighbors."

"Did you notice anything unusual about the crime scene? Besides the obvious, of course."

I forced myself to think past the horror of Thornton's dead eyes. "There was a piece of fabric caught on a branch. It looked expensive, like it had been torn from someone's clothing during a struggle."

Lance's hand had somehow found mine again, and now he pulled back abruptly, as if suddenly realizing what he'd been doing. He stood, putting distance between us. "She's answered enough questions for now. She's had a shock."

Martinez studied him for a long moment. "Agreed. Ms. Waters, I'll need you to come down to the station tomorrow to give a formal statement. Here's my card." He handed me a business card with his name and number. "Call if you remember anything else."

"I will." I took the card with numb fingers.

"Mr. Hendricks, a word?" Martinez jerked his head toward the crime scene.

Lance hesitated, glancing at me. "Will you be okay for a minute?"

I nodded, not trusting my voice.

The two men walked a short distance away, their voices too low for me to hear. I watched them, noting the way Lance stood with shoulders back, balanced on the balls of his feet, every inch the professional even in jeans and a t-shirt. Martinez spoke, gesturing toward the body, and Lance responded with sharp, economical movements.

They weren't just acquaintances. They'd worked together.

When Lance returned, his expression was carefully neutral. "Come on. I'll walk you home."

I stood on shaky legs, scooping up Minnie. The little Dachshund trembled against my chest. "What did Martinez want?"

"Just catching up." Lance's tone made it clear the subject was closed.

We walked in silence for the first block. My mind kept replaying the image of Thornton's body, the blood on the rock, the torn fabric. Someone had killed him. Someone had struck him hard enough to cave in his skull and left him in the bushes like trash.

"You're a cop," I said suddenly. "Or you were."

Lance's jaw tightened. "Military Police. Was."

"What happened?"

"I got hurt on the job. Medical leave until the brass decides if I'm fit for duty." His limp seemed more pronounced now, as if talking about it made it worse.

"Is that why you know Martinez?"

"We worked together on a case once before I transferred." He stopped at the entrance to Riverside Towers. "Listen, Crystal, you need to be careful.

Thornton was killed less than twenty-four hours after you inherited the property he wanted to buy. That's not a coincidence."

Ice slid down my spine. "You think I'm in danger?"

"I think you need to watch yourself. Keep your doors locked. Don't go walking alone after dark." His dark eyes bored into mine. "And if you notice anything unusual—anything at all—you call Martinez. Or me."

"Okay." My voice came out small.

His expression softened slightly. "You did well today. Most people panic at a crime scene. You kept your head and gave Martinez useful information."

"I didn't feel like I kept my head. I felt like I was falling apart."

"But you didn't." His hand lifted as if to touch my face, then dropped to his side. "Get some rest. Tomorrow's going to be a long day."

He turned and walked toward his apartment, King following obediently. I watched him go, my mind churning with questions. Who was Lance Hendricks really? And why did his professional mask slip every time he looked at me, only to slam back into place a moment later?

Inside my apartment, I locked the door and slid the chain into place. Minnie curled up on the couch, exhausted from the trauma of the day. I sat beside her, stroking her soft fur, and stared at Detective Martinez's card.

Richard Thornton was dead. Murdered. And somehow, I was tangled up in it.

The question was: why?

Chapter Four

"Did you hear?" Linda, four dogs straining on leashes in front of her, approached me.

I stood from where I planted fresh flowers in the common area, brushing dirt from my knees. The morning sun was already warm and sweat beaded on my forehead. I'd been out here for over an hour, trying to make the courtyard look more welcoming. Anything to keep my mind off finding Richard Thornton's body yesterday. "Hear what?"

Richard Thornton was found murdered!" Her eyes widened dramatically, as if she was sharing breaking news.

"Yes, I heard. I'm the one who found him. Or rather, Minnie did." I wiped my hands on the front of my jeans, leaving streaks of potting soil.

She gasped, pressing one hand to her chest while somehow maintaining control of four straining leashes. "How awful that must have been for you. I can't even imagine. Were you traumatized? Did you scream?"

"It was pretty bad." I didn't want to relive it, especially not with Linda, who would probably spread every detail to everyone at the dog park within the hour.

Betty Henderson, still in her robe and slippers, shuffled toward us from the direction of her apartment. Her white hair was barely combed, and she carried a steaming mug of what smelled like strong coffee. "You must be talking about Thornton. Terrible shame." She stepped back out of the way of the four dogs Linda walked, one of which was trying to sniff her slippers. "Can't you find a different job, dear? All those animals must be exhausting."

"I like the job I have, thank you." Linda scowled, yanking the dogs back into line.

"Well." Betty took a long sip of her coffee. "I heard, through the grapevine, mind you, that the suspect list is growing. I've only heard a couple of names, but one of them is you." She narrowed her eyes at Linda over the rim of her mug.

"Me?" Linda put a hand to her mouth. "Why would I be a suspect?"

Betty lowered her voice to what she probably thought was a whisper, but was still loud enough for half the courtyard to hear. "Because of the grudge you hold against him about the death of that dog. Everyone knows you blamed him for what happened to Buttercup."

"Anyone would be angry!" Linda's gaze moved to

me, her expression shifting from shock to accusation. "Did you say something to the police?"

I shifted uncomfortably, wishing I'd stayed inside my apartment this morning. "Uh...not just you. I mentioned Mark Shuford, too. I can't lie to the police." I glanced from her to Betty, then back again. "You would've done the same, right?"

"Maybe not if it meant someone getting into trouble that has no reason to be a suspect." She gripped the leashes tighter in her hand to pull the dogs away from where I'd just planted. One of them had been about to dig up my fresh petunias. "Shuford is the one they should really look at. After all, he has a motive stronger than any I might have."

"Like what?" An eager look came over Betty's face. She set down her coffee mug on the edge of the planter box and leaned in closer. "Do tell."

"I'm not one to spread gossip," Linda began, which immediately told me she was absolutely about to spread gossip, "but Mark was seen arguing violently with Thornton two days ago about financial ruin. My source, I won't say who, very clearly heard Mark tell Thornton that he would regret this...whatever this is."

"What kind of financial ruin?" I asked, despite myself. "What does Mark do?"

"He owns that new fusion restaurant downtown, aptly named Fusion. You know, the trendy place with the exposed brick?" Linda adjusted her grip on the leashes as a terrier pulled toward a nearby bush.

"Apparently, Thornton was blocking his expansion plans and spreading rumors about health code violations. Complete lies, of course, but enough to hurt business. Mark was facing bankruptcy."

Betty picked up her mug again, practically vibrating with interest. "I always thought that restaurant was too fancy for its own good. Twelve dollars for a side salad?"

"We shouldn't gossip." Still, I couldn't pull myself away from the conversation. It was like watching a car accident—horrible, but impossible to look away from.

"That's not all," Linda continued, clearly on a roll now. "Janet Hooper—no relation to me, thank goodness—the retired teacher in number 198, had a screaming match with Thornton at the dog park when he called animal control on her aggressive terrier. Animal control took the dog away from her." Her voice dropped. "The dog was euthanized. She was overheard saying that she hoped someone killed him. By him, she meant Thornton. Multiple witnesses heard it."

My chest tightened. Having your beloved pet euthanized because of someone's complaint? That would be devastating. "When did this happen?"

"Three days ago. The fight was in front of everyone at the park. Very public, very loud. Janet was beside herself." Linda's expression turned sympathetic for a moment before returning to gossipy excitement. "And that's not even the worst suspect."

I narrowed my eyes at her. "You're the source,

aren't you?"

"What makes you think that?" Linda's face flushed.

"Because you spend a lot of time at the dog park and could easily have overheard these conversations." And, by spreading this gossip, she could be trying to take the focus off herself. I didn't say that last part out loud.

"Pooh." She waved a dismissive hand, continuing as if I hadn't said anything. "Then, there's Jack Bradley, the environmental activist who has organized several protests about Thornton wanting to tear down Riverside Towers and the dog park to build an upscale hotel. Jack has been at every city council meeting for the past six months, making speeches about green spaces and wildlife habitats. He even chained himself to a tree last spring."

"I remember that!" Betty interjected. "It was in the paper. Police had to cut the chain."

"Exactly." Linda nodded. "And get this—Jack has a history. Eco-terrorism charges from his youth. He was acquitted, but still. The man has a violent past."

"I think you're making stuff up." Betty crossed her arms. "No one could have that many enemies."

"Thornton did." Linda hitched her chin as if to say, "What do you think about that?" She glanced past me. "Oh, there's Lance." She waved enthusiastically.

I saw my opportunity to escape the gossip session. "I need to speak to him. Excuse me." I made a mad dash across the courtyard and grabbed Lance's arm, practically dragging him into a hallway under a stairwell. King followed calmly, as if being pulled into dark corners was a regular occurrence. "Pretend we're having a conversation."

"We are having a conversation." A smile tugged at his lips. "What's going on?"

"Those two are the worst gossipers in the world." I proceeded to tell him about the conversation, detailing everything Linda had said about Mark Shuford, Janet Hooper, and Jack Bradley. When I finished, I frowned. "I'm just as bad, aren't I? I just told you everything that they said."

He laughed, a warm sound that made something flutter in my chest. "Maybe. But there's a difference between spreading gossip for entertainment and sharing potentially relevant information about a murder investigation. Have you gone to the station to file your report yet? Martinez might be interested in this 'gossip'." He made finger quotes around the last word.

"No, I haven't gone yet. Was going to go after I finished some things." I glanced down at my dirt-streaked jeans. "I'll go after I change."

"Want me to go with you?" His expression was neutral, but something in his tone suggested he genuinely wanted to help.

I shook my head, although it would be nice to have moral support. The idea of walking into a police station and talking about murder made my stomach churn. "I'm a big girl. Besides, I need to do some grocery shopping afterward. Thanks, though."

"Alright. But call me if you need anything." He pulled out his phone. "What's your number?"

After we exchanged numbers—a small moment that felt oddly significant—I headed to my apartment, fed Minnie, then changed into a clean pair of jeans and a blue blouse that made me look more put-together than I felt. Ten minutes later, I strolled into the police station, my palms sweating.

The building smelled like coffee and industrial cleaner. The front desk officer directed me to the second floor, where Detective Martinez's office was located. I found him behind a desk piled high with folders and paper coffee cups, his tie loosened, and his sleeves rolled up.

"Ms. Waters." He stood, gesturing to a chair across from his desk. "Thanks for coming in. Coffee?"

"No, thank you." I sat, clutching my purse in my lap.

"Let's start with your formal statement about finding the body." He pulled out a recording device. "Do you mind if I record this?"

"No, that's fine."

For the next twenty minutes, I walked through everything again—the walk around the lake, Minnie's behavior, finding Thornton's body, the 911 call. Martinez listened intently, occasionally asking clarifying questions. When I finished, he turned off the recorder.

"Now, was there something else you wanted to tell me?" His eyes were sharp, missing nothing.

I took a deep breath and repeated what Linda had told me, again detailing Mark Shuford's argument with Thornton, Janet Hooper's public confrontation, and Jack Bradley's activism.

Martinez wrote everything down, his expression thoughtful. "Mark Shuford. I'm familiar with him. We've already spoken to him about his whereabouts the night of the murder."

"And?"

"I can't share details of an ongoing investigation, but let's just say his alibi is shaky." Martinez tapped his pen against his notebook. "What about Janet Hooper? Did your source mention where she was that night?"

"Linda didn't say. She just mentioned the confrontation at the dog park." I hesitated. "Is it true that her dog was euthanized?"

"Yes. Three days ago. Animal control determined the dog showed aggressive behavior toward children and other animals. Mrs. Hooper blamed Thornton for the complaint, though there were multiple complaints filed over several months." Martinez's expression softened. "Losing a pet is traumatic. People don't always think clearly when they're grieving."

"What about Jack Bradley?"

"The environmental activist." Martinez flipped through his notes. "He's definitely on our radar. He was at the park the night of the murder, though he claims he left before nine PM. We're working on verifying that."

A chill ran down my spine. "He was there? The night Thornton was killed?"

"According to his statement, he walks the trails every evening. Says it helps him think." Martinez studied my face. "Does that concern you?"

"I don't know. Maybe?" I twisted my purse strap in my hands. "It just seems like a lot of people had reasons to hate Thornton."

"That's the problem with victims like Richard Thornton. Developers who step on people to get what they want tend to accumulate enemies." Martinez closed his notebook. "Is there anything else you can think of? Any detail, no matter how small?"

I thought back to the crime scene, forcing myself to remember. "The torn fabric on the branch. Have you identified what it was from?"

"Expensive suit jacket. Italian wool. We're working on tracing it." He stood, signaling the end of our meeting. "If you think of anything else, call me immediately. And Ms. Waters? Be careful. Whoever killed Thornton is still out there."

The weight of his words followed me out of the station and through my grocery shopping. I moved through the aisles in a daze, barely paying attention to what I was putting in my cart. When I got home, I realized I'd bought three boxes of the same cereal and no milk.

I was unpacking groceries when someone knocked on my door. I checked the peephole and saw Lance, holding two cups of coffee.

"Hi." He held up the cups when I opened the door. "Thought you might need this after your trip to the station."

"You have no idea." I stepped back to let him in. King immediately went to greet Minnie, who, for once, didn't snap but actually wagged her tail. "How did you know I was back?"

"I saw you pull into the parking lot from my window." He handed me a cup. "Not creepy, I promise. I just wanted to make sure you were okay."

We sat at my small kitchen table, the afternoon sun streaming through the window. For a moment, neither of us spoke. The silence was awkward, stilted. Lance seemed out of practice with casual conversation, his shoulders tense, his coffee cup held in both hands as if he needed something to do with them.

"So." I took a sip of coffee. Perfect—cream, no sugar, exactly how I liked it. Had I mentioned that to him, or was he observant enough to have noticed? "Martinez seemed interested in what Linda told me."

"I'm not surprised. The gossip mill usually has at least a kernel of truth." He studied me over his cup. "How are you holding up?"

"Honestly? I'm terrified." The admission came out before I could stop it. "I inherited this place less than a week ago, and now there's a murder investigation, and apparently Thornton wanted to buy Riverside Towers, and what if the killer thinks I'm in the way, too? I still can't get rid of the nagging feeling that my aunt's death might not have been an accident."

Lance set down his coffee and leaned forward, his expression serious. "Listen to me. You're not in danger. Thornton's murder was personal—the level of violence, the location, everything about it suggests someone who knew him and hated him. You didn't even know the man."

"But I own something he wanted."

"Wanted past tense. He's dead. Whatever plans he had died with him." Lance's tone was firm and confident. "But if it makes you feel better, I'm right across the courtyard. You have my number. Anything seems off, you call me immediately."

"Why are you being so nice to me?" The question came out more vulnerable than I'd intended.

He was quiet for a long moment, something flickering across his face—emotion quickly shuttered away. "Because you remind me that not everything is dark. And because someone should look out for you while you're figuring all this out."

The moment stretched between us, charged with something I couldn't quite name. His dark eyes held mine, and I saw past the professional mask to something softer underneath. Then, just as quickly, it was gone. He pulled back, emotional walls slamming into place.

"I should go." He stood abruptly. "Early morning tomorrow."

"Lance—"

"Get some rest, Crystal." His voice was gentle but final. He called King and headed for the door, pausing with his hand on the handle. "Lock this behind me."

After he left, I sat at my table and stared at my half-finished coffee. Lance Hendricks was a puzzle—all hard edges and professional distance, except for those brief moments when something else showed through. Something that made my heart race and my thoughts scatter.

I locked the door as he'd instructed, checking it twice, then curled up on the couch with Minnie. Three suspects. Mark Shuford, facing financial ruin. Janet Hooper, grieving her euthanized dog. Jack Bradley, the environmental activist with a violent past.

One of them had killed Richard Thornton.

The question was: which one?

Chapter Five

Forgoing the dog park again, heart in my throat, I took Minnie to the walking path. The thought of running into someone—anyone—who might want to discuss Thornton's murder made my stomach twist. I needed peace, not more gossip.

My steps faltered as we drew close to the place where Minnie had found Thornton's body. The yellow crime scene tape remained, a stark reminder of that day's horror. It snapped and fluttered in the breeze like some macabre decoration.

I squared my shoulders and marched past the spot, refusing to look too closely at the trampled grass or the dark stain I could see from the corner of my eye. What was needed was a good, prolonged rain to wash the spot clean.

The long path would lead me along a creek that I was sure would soothe me. Water had always calmed my nerves, ever since I was a little girl visiting Aunt

Mary Jane and playing by the fountain in her courtyard.

The path narrowed as it wound deeper into the woods, the canopy of leaves overhead creating a tunnel of dappled green light. My footsteps crunched on fallen twigs and last year's leaves. The air smelled of earth and growing things.

By the time the sound of water babbling over rocks reached me, my heart had settled into a more normal rhythm. The tension in my shoulders eased, and I could breathe deeply again without feeling like I might cry. I let Minnie off her leash and sat on a large boulder near the creek's edge. Sunlight kissed the top of the water with glints of diamonds. A slight breeze rustled the tree branches. A bird called to its mate, a sweet trill that echoed through the trees. What a gorgeous day. I closed my eyes and raised my face to the sun, letting the warmth seep into my skin.

For a few precious moments, I could pretend that everything was normal. That I was just a woman enjoying a walk with her dog, not someone who'd discovered a murder victim less than forty-eight hours ago.

Minnie whined, then growled, deep in her throat.

My eyes snapped open, my brief peace shattered.

She dug under a bush near the water, her paws working frantically at the soft earth.

"Okay, girl. Whatever it is you're terrorizing, leave it alone." I pushed to my feet, brushing dirt from the seat of my jeans, then parted the branches. Probably just an interesting scent or a small animal burrow.

A white coffee cup with gold trim lay half buried in the dirt and leaf litter. The cup was pristine white porcelain, clearly expensive, with an elegant gold band around the rim. A coral-colored lipstick left a perfect imprint on the edge, as if someone had just set it down moments ago rather than long enough for it to be partially buried. Since it was nicer than anything my aunt had left me, and certainly nicer than anything I'd ever owned, I stored it in my backpack. Someone had probably dropped it during a picnic or romantic walk. I could wash it and add it to my sparse collection of nice dishes.

I didn't think anything of it until I found a broken cell phone with a cracked screen a few feet away, partially hidden under a fallen log. The screen was spiderwebbed with cracks, and the back casing was dented, as if it had been thrown or dropped from a height. Then, just beyond the phone, I spotted a pair of footprints too big to belong to a woman, pressed deep into the muddy bank near the water's edge. The tread pattern was clear—work boots, maybe size ten or eleven.

My heart started racing again. This wasn't just random litter.

I frowned and carefully lined up the phone and the cup next to the footprints, being careful not to disturb anything, before snapping photos with my cell phone. Could be nothing, might be something. I sure hoped it was nothing. But the location nagged at me. Why would someone abandon an expensive phone and designer cup out here?

I glanced back up the trail, trying to orient myself. We had to be a football field away from where Thornton was killed, maybe more. The path curved and twisted, but generally followed the creek downstream. But that didn't mean that whoever killed him hadn't come this way. Maybe they'd fled along the creek, away from the main path where they might be spotted.

The coffee cup threw me, though. Why bring a designer cup to a hiking trail? Didn't most people carry a thermos when taking a walk? Or those insulated travel mugs with lids? A delicate porcelain cup with gold trim seemed completely impractical for outdoor recreation unless someone hadn't been planning a hike. Unless they'd been meeting someone.

My imagination started working overtime. Had Thornton met his killer here? Had they walked together to the spot where he died? Or had someone else been here, someone who'd witnessed something and fled in panic?

Shaking off the thoughts, I hooked the leash back on Minnie and resumed our walk. Thornton's death was up to the police to solve, not me. I was a property manager, not a detective. However, I couldn't help but wonder whether I should call Martinez about what I'd found. But then again, it might be nothing. I didn't want to waste police time on what could be ordinary litter.

The path continued to wind through the woods, gradually climbing upward away from the creek. Minnie seemed content now, trotting along with her nose to the ground, tail wagging. Whatever she'd sensed earlier had passed.

The yapping of dogs ahead caused Minnie to strain against her leash, her ears perking forward with interest. A few minutes later, we stepped into a clearing where a small cabin stood, rustic but well-maintained with a wraparound porch and cheerful red shutters. A middle-aged woman wearing a frilly apron over jeans tossed a ball to a herd of Dachshunds—at least eight of them, all different colors and coat types, racing and tumbling over each other in pursuit of the toy.

I smiled and headed her way, my worries temporarily forgotten. To me, there was nothing cuter than Dachshunds playing. Their short legs and long bodies made everything they did look comical and adorable. My heart skipped a beat when I spotted the sign leaning against the porch railing: "Dachshund Puppies For Sale - Health Guaranteed - AKC Registered."

"May I see the puppies?" I called out, unable to contain my enthusiasm.

"Sure, you can." She bent down to pet Minnie, who wagged her tail instead of growling. "What a sweet girl. How old is she?"

"Three years old. I've had her since she was ten weeks."

"She's beautiful." The woman straightened, wiping her hands on her apron. "I'm Margaret, by the way. I've got miniatures, standard, long-haired, and short. These dogs make me happy. I breed them to make others happy. Come on in." She led us up two steps and into a clean home that smelled of dog—not unpleasant, just distinctly canine—and vanilla air freshener. A baby gate separated the puppies from the carpeted living room.

Through the gate, I could see at least a dozen puppies in various stages of play and sleep. Some wrestled with each other, others gnawed on toys, and a few were curled up in a fluffy dog bed.

My eyes fell first on an adorable long-haired red and white piebald who was trying to climb over her littermates to get to the gate. Her fur was silky and her eyes bright with curiosity. Then I spotted a frisky, chocolate-colored short-haired dog who pulled a rope toy three times her size across the floor. "Oh, my gosh." I climbed over the gate, dropped to my knees, and was immediately overcome by puppies jumping up and licking my face. Their tiny paws scrabbled against my jeans, and their puppy breath was warm and sweet.

I picked up the red and white piebald, who immediately snuggled into my arms. Then the chocolate wiggled its way onto my lap, not to be outdone. They were perfect. Both of them.

"How much are they?" I asked, already knowing I couldn't leave without them.

"Since I can see how much you love the breed," Margaret said with a knowing smile, "I'll let you have them for $400 each. That includes their first round of shots and a health certificate from my vet."

I quickly calculated how much was left in my bank account. I'd been paid out for my vacation time when I quit my job at the school, and I hadn't touched my aunt's accounts yet while the estate was being settled. I could afford this. Barely. "Do you take checks?"

"Sure do." The woman smiled and nodded. "Give me your address, and I'll mail you their papers as soon as I have them. It should be about two weeks. They're eight weeks old today, so they're ready to go home."

I happily wrote the check, my hand shaking slightly with excitement, and loaded the puppies into a cardboard box Margaret provided, lined with soft towels. I'd already named the red-and-white one Daisy, after my favorite flower, and the chocolate one Clarabelle, after the cow in the old Disney cartoons Aunt Mary Jane used to let me watch. I now had Minnie and her two best friends. Poor Minnie did not look happy as we headed home, her ears pinned back as she stared at the box with deep suspicion, but I knew she'd adjust soon enough. She just needed time.

The walk back seemed longer with the box in my arms. The puppies were surprisingly heavy, and they kept moving around, making the box awkward to carry. By the time Riverside Towers came into view, my arms ached from holding the box and sweat beaded on my forehead despite the pleasant temperature. I'd never been so happy to see anyone in my life as I was to see Lance on a ladder painting trim around a window on the second floor.

He spotted me and climbed down, setting his paintbrush on the tray. "You've got your hands full."

"I couldn't resist." I grinned and held out the box so he could peek inside. "Do you mind? My arms are about to fall off."

"Not at all." He relieved me of the box, barely seeming to notice the weight. His arms didn't even strain. "You're going to have your hands full with three dogs. Have you ever raised puppies before?"

"Yes, Minnie. It'll be fun."

"It'll be a lot of work," he corrected, but his tone was amused rather than critical. "Potty training, chewing, crying at night..."

"Don't ruin my excitement with reality." The grin never left my face until I spotted a sheet of white paper waving at me from my front door, tucked under the knocker. Written in bold black letters that looked like they'd been made with a thick marker were the words: "Keep Your Nose Out." A strong whiff of perfume drifted on the breeze.

My smile died. My stomach dropped.

Lance stopped me from ripping it down, his hand catching my wrist. "Don't touch it. Let's get these pups inside and call Martinez."

"You think this is about Thornton?" My voice came out higher than I intended.

"Don't you?" He tilted his head, his expression serious. "What else have you been meddling in?"

"I haven't been meddling in anything. I didn't choose to find a dead body." Anger flared in my chest, hot and defensive. "I was just walking my dog. I didn't ask to be involved in any of this."

"I know." His voice gentled. "But someone thinks you're too involved. Or they're worried you might become too involved."

My hands shook as I unlocked the door, careful not to touch the note. The cheerful yapping of the puppies in the box seemed incongruous with the threat on my door. Lance set the box down gently in the living room, and the puppies immediately started trying to climb out.

"Stay here with them." Lance pulled out his phone. "I'm calling Martinez."

I sank onto the couch, watching Minnie cautiously approach the box. Daisy poked her head up, and Minnie's tail gave a tentative wag. Maybe everything would be okay. Perhaps this was just someone trying to scare me.

But as I looked at the note still fluttering on my door, visible through the open doorway, I couldn't shake the feeling that things were about to get much worse before they got better.

Lance's voice was low and urgent as he spoke to

Martinez. "Yeah, she's fine, but you need to see this. Someone left a threatening note on her door... No, she hasn't touched it... We'll wait here."

He ended the call and looked at me, his dark eyes filled with concern. "Martinez is on his way. And Crystal?" He sat down beside me, close enough that I could feel the warmth radiating from him. "Until we know who killed Thornton and why, you need to be very, very careful."

I nodded, unable to speak past the lump in my throat. In the box beside us, three Dachshunds yapped and played, blissfully unaware that their new owner might be in danger.

Chapter Six

All three dachshunds set up a frenzy of barking when someone knocked on my door early the next morning. The sound was deafening in my small apartment, three different pitches of yapping creating a cacophony that made my head throb. With a frown, I carried my barely touched coffee—my precious first cup that I desperately needed—and opened the door.

A stylish woman with her bleached blond hair in a French twist stood outside my door, looking like she'd stepped out of a fashion magazine. Her makeup was flawless, her posture perfect, and her designer suit probably cost more than three months of my old salary. Her smile looked forced, tight around the edges. "Ms. Waters?"

"Yes. May I help you?" She didn't look like a resident of the complex. Far too upscale. Our tenants leaned more toward the comfortable-casual end of the spectrum.

"I'm Victoria Thornton. I heard you found my husband's...body." Her voice caught slightly on the last word, though whether from genuine emotion or practiced effect, I couldn't tell.

My stomach dropped. Richard Thornton's wife. Ex-wife? I wasn't sure. "Oh. Yes. Please, come in." I stepped back to allow her entrance, suddenly very aware of the clutter in my living room. Aunt Mary Jane's doilies and figurines still covered every surface, and now puppy toys were scattered across the floor.

The three dogs sniffed at her expensive Italian leather shoes. I'd seen those exact shoes in a magazine once, priced at over eight hundred dollars. Just for shoes. Minnie growled deep in her throat, her hackles rising slightly. That was unusual. Minnie might be timid around other dogs, but she typically liked people.

"Excuse me." I set my cup of coffee on the crowded coffee table, barely finding space between a porcelain shepherdess and a stack of tenant complaint forms, and scooped Minnie into my arms. Daisy and Bella immediately started yapping louder, as if protesting being left out. "Make yourself at home. I'll be right back." I carried Minnie to the bedroom while the other two followed, their little legs pumping as they tried to keep up. Once they were comfortable on my bed—already starting to chew on the decorative pillows I'd never liked anyway—I returned to the living room.

Victoria perched on the edge of the sofa as if she might soil her expensive suit just by sitting fully on the furniture. Her eyebrows arched as she glanced around the apartment, taking in the outdated decor with barely concealed disdain. Her nose wrinkled slightly.

Heat crept up my neck. "I haven't had time to change things since taking over here. Can I get you a cup of coffee?" I gestured toward my small kitchen.

"No, thank you, but please, go ahead and finish yours." She waved a manicured hand toward my cup, her nails painted a perfect coral that matched her lipstick exactly. Where had I seen that shade before?

Thank you, Lord. I couldn't start my day without one or two cups. Or three. I picked up my cup, sat in a chair across from her, and peered over the rim. "Is there something I can help you with?"

Victoria smoothed her skirt, a nervous gesture that seemed at odds with her polished appearance. "Yes, actually." She crossed her ankles, her posture finishing-school perfect. "I'd like to ask that you honor Richard's memory by keeping the park open. He loved that park. Loved seeing families and their pets enjoying the outdoors. It would devastate him to know it might close."

I stared at her with my mouth full of coffee before swallowing hard, nearly choking. "I'm not the one who wanted to close the park. Richard was. From my aunt's records, he also wanted to tear down Riverside Towers and this entire neighborhood to build luxury condos." I set my cup down carefully, trying to keep my voice level. "Your husband was the threat to the park, not me."

"No, you must be mistaken." She shook her head, her French twist not moving an inch. She gave another forced smile that didn't reach her eyes. "My Richard was always about helping those not as blessed as he was. Community service was his passion. He donated to the animal shelter every year and sponsored youth sports teams. The idea that he would destroy a public park is absurd."

I opened my mouth to argue, then closed it again. Either she was delusional about her husband's character, or she was lying. But why? "Mrs. Thornton—"

"Victoria, please."

"Victoria. I'm sorry for your loss, but I think you have the wrong information about your husband's business dealings. I have documentation—"

"I'm sure it's all a misunderstanding." Victoria got to her feet abruptly, cutting me off. "Please consider my request. Richard would have wanted the park preserved. It's the least we can do to honor his memory." Then, as if I hadn't told her she had her facts completely wrong, she waltzed out my front door, her heels clicking sharply on the concrete walkway.

I stood in my doorway, watching her go, baffled by the conversation. What just happened?

Before I could close the door behind her, Linda rushed over from across the courtyard, straining to control a massive Great Dane on a leash. The dog was nearly as tall as she was and seemed determined to drag her in every direction at once. "Was that Victoria Thornton?"

"Yes. She asked me to keep the dog park open as if I had the power to do that." I stared after the woman as she climbed into a silver Mercedes parked in the visitor lot. "She seemed to be grieving her husband's death."

"That doesn't make sense." Linda wrestled the Great Dane away from my flower beds. "They were divorced. A very bitter divorce. She received a 3 million dollar settlement two years ago. The two hated each other. Richard tried to contest the settlement, claiming she was having an affair. It was all over the society pages."

I frowned. "She called him 'my Richard' and acted like they were still married."

"I wonder what she's playing at?" Linda's eyes lit up with that familiar gossip gleam. "You need to find out whether she was in town when Richard was killed. What if she's the murderer? Maybe she wanted more money from him, or revenge for something."

I narrowed my eyes. "That isn't my place. I have enough work to do here without traipsing about trying to find out who murdered someone." Not to mention the fact that I'd already received a warning note telling me to keep my nose out of things. That note was currently in Detective Martinez's evidence locker, and I had no desire to receive another one. Or something worse.

"I should be angry with you for putting my name out there as a suspect," Linda said, her expression shifting to something more magnanimous, "but I've decided to forgive you and help you solve this." She grinned as if she'd just offered me the world's greatest gift.

Was no one listening to me today? "I'm not going to solve anything except why the garbage disposal in apartment 104 spews the garbage out instead of keeping it down." Lance had mentioned he would be gone most of the morning handling some personal business, so I'd have to take a look myself and fill him in when he returned. "Excuse me." I retrieved my toolbox from inside the front door, then headed to apartment 104.

The door opened before I could knock. A woman in her mid-sixties with iron-gray hair pulled into a tight bun answered with a scowl on her face that looked permanently etched into her features. "I thought you were going to stand outside and talk all day."

"No, ma'am. Just taking care of business." I tried to smile, though my patience was already wearing thin from the strange morning. I headed for the kitchen and stared into a sink full of crusted-on...stuff. Brown, slimy, unidentifiable stuff that made my stomach turn. "How long has it not been working?"

"A week." The woman—Mrs. Snyder, according to her lease, which I'd checked before coming over, crossed her arms over her housedress. "It sure seems to take a lot of time to get help around here. When your aunt ran the place, she handled things promptly. I called three days ago."

Guilt twisted in my gut. I'd been so caught up in the murder investigation and getting my new puppies settled that I'd let some work orders slip. "I apologize for the delay. Let's get this fixed right now."

"Hmmm." Mrs. Snyder didn't look appeased.

I set my toolbox on the counter, then turned on the faucet, watching the water fill the sink and swirl around the drain without going down. Here goes nothing. I hit the switch for the garbage disposal.

Gunk and water formed a geyser that spewed from the sink, drenching me with a smell like rotting vegetables mixed with something that might once have been meat. The smell was overwhelming, like someone had opened a dumpster in July. I stumbled back into the refrigerator, slamming into it hard enough to rattle the contents. A large, painted pickle jar that had been balanced on top crashed to the floor, hitting with an explosion of glass and coins.

"For heaven's sake!" Mrs. Snyder clasped the collar of her blouse and jumped back. "You're a walking disaster zone." She reached over and turned off the faucet, mercifully stopping the geyser.

I stood there, dripping and reeking, coins and glass shards scattered around my feet. "I think there is something stuck in there." I got to my feet carefully, trying not to step on any glass. "If you get a broom, I'll clean up the coins and glass, then see how to unclog the disposal." I pulled my phone from my pocket—thankfully still dry—and googled "how to unclog garbage disposal."

"Of course, there's something stuck. I dropped a plastic fork down there last week. Hasn't worked right since." She left and returned with a broom and dustpan, handing them to me as if I'd been the one to make the mess.

"A plastic fork?" I tried to keep the exasperation out of my voice. "Why didn't you just reach in and pull it out?"

"That's disgusting. That's what I pay rent for. To have someone else do those things."

I counted to ten. Then twenty. "Do you have the little wrench thing that came with the disposal?" It was getting harder to maintain my friendly attitude and readiness to help. Much harder.

"Check the drawer to the right of the sink." Mrs. Snyder took the broom back and started sweeping coins and glass into the dustpan and dropping them all on top of the kitchen table with little clinks and clatters. "I'm saving for a cruise." Once she had the coins spread out on the table—it had to be at least forty or fifty dollars in change—and the glass shards thrown away, she dug in the cupboards for something to put her savings into. "You should go home and take a shower. You stink."

I rolled my eyes where she couldn't see me, read the step-by-step instructions on my phone about how to unclog and unlock the disposal, and found the Allen wrench in the drawer. Following the instructions, I inserted the wrench into the hole at the bottom of the disposal and turned it back and forth to dislodge whatever was stuck. After a few minutes of effort, I felt it give. Then I reached up into the disposal—trying not to think about how disgusting this was—and pulled out the mangled plastic fork. And voila! I turned on the water and flipped the switch. Worked like a charm. The water drained smoothly, and the disposal hummed without spewing anything.

In place of a thank you, Mrs. Snyder informed me to bring her a new pickle jar if I found one. "The ones this size aren't easy to find. I've been using that one for fifteen years."

"I'll keep an eye out." I couldn't get out of her apartment fast enough. The woman was right about one thing, though. I reeked of food that had been sitting in her disposal for who knows how long.

I trudged across the courtyard, drawing stares from a couple of residents sitting by the pool. One woman wrinkled her nose and moved her chair farther away.

"Hey." Lance strolled up the sidewalk, back earlier than expected. He stopped when he got within ten feet of me, then sniffed. His eyes widened. "What happened? Did something die on you?"

With a sigh, I told him about fixing the disposal and Mrs. Snyder's charming personality. "My morning had already started off weird when Victoria Thornton visited me. Asked me not to close down the dog park. I told her I had nothing to do with that. Plus, Minnie didn't seem to like her at all, and Minnie likes everyone except other dogs." I kept walking toward my apartment, leaving him to follow at what I'm sure was a more comfortable distance. "According to Linda, Victoria and Richard were divorced. Bitter divorce. Three million dollar settlement."

"Dogs are often a good judge of character." He put a hand up to his nose, clearly trying to be subtle about it but failing.

"Do I really smell that bad?"

He nodded, his eyes twinkling with barely suppressed amusement. "Pretty rank. Like a dumpster in August. But good job on fixing the disposal. You'll make a regular handy girl someday."

"Not as long as I can hire someone or convince you to do it." I shot him a look. "I don't mind the bookkeeping part of running the complex, but fixing anything will only be because I absolutely have to." I unlocked my door, trying to ignore how his presence made my pulse quicken even when I smelled like garbage. "Do you know Victoria?"

"I've run across her a time or two." His smile faded, his expression becoming guarded.

I tilted my head, studying his face. "Why do I get the feeling you might know her better than that?"

He heaved a sigh, running a hand through his dark hair. "She's been asking me to dinner a few times over the past year. I keep turning her down. She doesn't take rejection well. Last time she showed up at my apartment with wine and candles."

Heat flared in my chest. Jealousy? No, that was ridiculous. "She's very pretty," I said, trying to sound casual.

"Not my type." He met my eyes directly. "I like my girls...simpler. More genuine. Less..." He waved a hand as if searching for words. "Less calculating." With a flash of a grin that made my stomach flip, he walked away whistling.

I stood in my doorway, dripping garbage disposal gunk, watching him go. I still thought there was a story to tell there. A story I very much wanted to hear.

Inside, three dachshunds greeted me with enthusiastic yapping, and I realized that despite the warning note, the strange visit from Victoria, and being covered in rotting food, I was happier than I'd been in years.

Even if I did desperately need a shower.

Chapter Seven

I was teaching Daisy and Bella not to chew on my favorite throw pillows when I noticed the white envelope that had been slipped under my door. My stomach dropped. The last time I'd received an unexpected note, it had been a warning to keep my nose out of things.

With trembling hands, I set the puppies down and picked up the envelope. No name, no postage, just plain white paper. I opened it carefully, as if it might explode.

Block letters, written in the same thick black marker as before: "STOP ASKING QUESTIONS OR YOU'LL BE NEXT."

The paper slipped from my fingers and fluttered to the floor. Minnie trotted over and sniffed it, then looked up at me with concern in her dark eyes.

"I haven't been asking questions," I said aloud to the empty room, my voice shaking. "I've been fixing garbage disposals and buying puppies and trying to mind my own business."

But that wasn't entirely true, was it? I'd talked to Martinez about the suspects. I'd found those items by the creek and taken photos. I'd mentioned them to Lance, who'd probably told Martinez. And I'd been gossiping with Linda and Betty about everyone connected to Thornton.

Someone thought I knew too much. Or was getting too close to something.

I scooped up all three dogs, grabbed my phone and keys, and practically ran across the courtyard to Lance's apartment. Since my arms were full of squirming Dachshunds, I kicked at the door.

King's bark echoed from inside, followed by Lance's voice telling him to settle. The door opened, and Lance stood there in sweatpants and a t-shirt, his hair damp from a recent shower. His expression shifted immediately from casual to alert when he saw my face.

"What's wrong?"

I thrust the note at him, unable to speak past the lump in my throat.

He read it quickly, his jaw tightening. "When did you get this?"

"Just now. Someone slipped it under my door." I stepped inside without being invited, needing to be somewhere that felt safe. The puppies wriggled in my arms, trying to get down to investigate this new space.

Lance closed the door behind me and locked it—

both the handle and the deadbolt. "Did you see anyone in the courtyard?"

"No. I was playing with the puppies and didn't notice the note until a few minutes ago. It could have been there for an hour or five minutes." I set the dogs down, and they immediately started sniffing everything. King watched them with patient tolerance.

"We need to call Martinez." Lance was already pulling out his phone.

"Again?" I sank onto his couch, which was surprisingly comfortable and far less cluttered than mine. His apartment was neat, minimalist even, with just a couch, a coffee table, a TV, and a bookshelf full of what looked like police procedural novels and military thrillers. "He's going to think I'm making this up for attention."

"No, he won't. This is the second threat you've received in two days." Lance sat beside me, close enough that I could smell his soap—something clean and masculine. "Someone is escalating. First a warning, now a direct threat. That's not a good sign."

Detective Martinez arrived twenty minutes later, his expression grim as he examined the note through an evidence bag. "Same handwriting as the first one. Block letters, black marker. Probably used gloves, but we'll test for prints anyway. I assume we'll find both of yours?"

I nodded. "What am I supposed to do?" I asked, hearing the desperation in my own voice. "Just wait for them to make good on the threat?"

"No." Martinez looked at Lance. "She shouldn't be alone right now. Not until we have a better handle on who's behind this."

"I'll keep an eye on her," Lance said immediately.

"I don't need a babysitter," I protested, though the idea of being alone in my apartment with a would-be killer lurking around Riverside Towers terrified me. "I have three dogs. They'll protect me."

Both men looked at my dachshunds, who were currently wrestling over a chew toy, their stubby legs tangling together as they rolled across Lance's floor.

"Right," Martinez said dryly. "Fierce protectors."

"Minnie growled at Victoria Thornton," I pointed out. "They can at least give me a warning." Not that they had when the note arrived.

"Did she now?" Martinez pulled out his notebook. "Tell me about that visit."

I recounted Victoria's strange conversation about keeping the park open and honoring Richard's memory, her insistence that he'd been a philanthropist despite all evidence to the contrary. Martinez wrote it all down, his expression thoughtful.

"Victoria Thornton has an alibi for the night of the murder," he said. "She was at a charity gala in San Francisco with about three hundred witnesses. But that doesn't mean she couldn't have hired someone."

A chill ran down my spine. "You think she's behind the threats?"

"I think she's someone we need to look at more closely." Martinez tucked his notebook away. "In the meantime, you need to be careful. No more walks alone. No answering the door without checking who it is first. And if anything else happens, anything at all, you call me immediately."

After Martinez left, I gathered up my puppies. "I should get back to my apartment. I have work to do."

"Not alone, you're not." Lance stood, grabbing King's leash. "I'm walking you back. And from now on, I'm walking you and Minnie whenever you need to go out. No arguments."

"Lance—"

"Crystal." He met my eyes, his expression serious. "Someone threatened to kill you. This isn't a game. Until we know who's behind this and why, you're not taking any chances."

The intensity in his voice made my breath catch. "Okay," I whispered.

We walked the short distance to my apartment, Lance's presence solid and reassuring beside me. He checked inside before letting me enter, even looking in the closets and bathroom like he expected someone to jump out at us.

"Lock this behind me," he instructed. "I'll come get you at five for the evening walk with the dogs."

True to his word, Lance knocked on my door at exactly five o'clock. I'd spent the afternoon attempting to work on tenant files while trying not to think about the threat or imagine killers hiding in every shadow. The puppies had been a helpful distraction, requiring nearly constant attention and supervision.

"Ready?" Lance asked when I opened the door. His gaze landed on the dog sling over my shoulder.

"Bella refuses to walk on a leash." I clipped Minnie and Daisy's leashes to their harnesses and stepped outside. The evening air was pleasant, cooler than earlier, with the sun starting to dip toward the horizon. Under different circumstances, it would have been a lovely evening for a walk.

"Let's skip the walking path today." My stomach churned at the thought of returning to where I'd found Thornton's body. "Just stick to the dog park?"

"Good idea." Lance's hand rested casually on my lower back as we walked, a gesture that felt both protective and intimate. I had to admit that I liked the feel of his hand on my back.

The dog park was busier than usual, with at least a dozen dogs running around and their owners chatting in small groups. I recognized a few faces from previous visits. Linda was there with her collection of dogs, and she waved enthusiastically when she saw us.

"Twice in one week!" she called out. "You're becoming a regular."

"Just getting the dogs some exercise." I unclipped the leashes once we were safely inside the small dog enclosure and let Bella out of her sling.

Minnie immediately pressed against my leg and

refused to move. I sighed. Some things never changed. Daisy and Bella, on the other hand, ran around like they were on speed or something.

Lance stood beside me, his gaze scanning the park with what I was beginning to recognize as professional assessment. He wasn't just looking. He was observing. Cataloging faces, noting exits, watching for anything unusual. The cop in him was fully engaged.

"You miss it, don't you?" I asked quietly. "Police work."

"Every day." His voice was rough. "Being on leave feels like...like I'm not who I'm supposed to be anymore."

"What happened? If you don't mind me asking."

He was quiet for so long, I thought he wouldn't answer. Finally, he said, "I was chasing a suspect through an abandoned building. Fell through a rotted floor. Landed on rebar." He touched his leg, where I'd noticed the limp. "Tore up my knee pretty badly. Three surgeries later, and the doctors still aren't sure if I'll pass the physical fitness requirements to return to active duty."

"I'm sorry." The words felt inadequate.

"The worst part isn't the injury. It's the waiting. Not knowing if I'll ever get back to doing what I'm good at." He looked down at me, something vulnerable in his expression. "But this—helping you, protecting you—it feels like I have a purpose again."

My heart squeezed. "Lance—"

King's sudden bark cut me off. The German Shepherd had been lying calmly by Lance's feet, but now he stood rigid, his attention focused on something beyond the fence. A low growl rumbled in his chest.

Lance's entire demeanor changed. "Stay here," he commanded, his voice sharp with authority.

"What? Why?"

But he was already moving, King at his side, toward a figure standing in the shadows near the tree line. I squinted, trying to make out who it was. Male, average height, wearing a dark hoodie despite the warm evening. He'd been watching us.

The moment Lance started toward him, the figure bolted.

"Police! Stop!" Lance's voice rang out across the park, and several dog owners turned to stare.

But the figure had already disappeared into the trees. Lance pursued, running with a slight hitch in his gait from his injured knee, King racing ahead. They vanished into the shadows.

My heart pounded. I bent to scoop up Minnie, who was shaking, and rushed to the fence. Linda appeared at my elbow.

"What's happening? Who was that?"

"I don't know." My voice came out thin and scared. "Someone was watching us."

Several tense minutes passed before Lance emerged from the trees, breathing hard, King panting beside him. His expression was frustrated.

"Lost him. He had a car parked on the access road." Lance pulled out his phone, presumably to call Martinez. "Dark sedan, couldn't get the plates."

Linda's eyes went wide. "Oh my God. Someone followed you here? Crystal, you need to be careful. The killer is targeting you!"

"Linda, please," I said, but she was already spreading the news to the other dog owners, creating a ripple of concerned conversation throughout the park.

Lance finished his call and returned to me, his hand finding mine and squeezing. "We're leaving. Now."

He kept me close as we walked back to Riverside Towers. His gaze constantly scanned our surroundings. King walked slightly ahead, alert and protective. My three dachshunds seemed to sense the tension and stayed quiet.

"You're staying at my place tonight," Lance said as we entered the complex. It wasn't a question.

"Lance, I can't—"

"Yes, you can. Someone is following you, Crystal. Someone who's already killed once and threatened you twice. I'm not letting you stay alone."

Part of me wanted to argue, to insist I could take care of myself. But the truth was, I was terrified. "Okay," I agreed quietly. "But the dogs come with me."

Relief flashed across his face. "Good. Pack an overnight bag. I'll wait outside your door."

Twenty minutes later, I was settled on Lance's

couch with my three dogs and an overnight bag. He'd given me a pillow and blanket, insisting I take the bed while he slept out here, but I'd refused. The couch was comfortable enough, and besides, I felt safer in the living room where I could hear him moving around.

"Thank you," I said as he handed me a cup of tea. "For everything."

"Don't thank me yet. We still need to figure out who's behind this." He sat in the armchair across from me, King at his feet. "Tomorrow, we're going to Martinez with everything you've observed. Every conversation, every strange interaction. Someone is scared of what you might know or figure out. If you go over everything again, you might remember something you missed."

"But I don't know anything," I protested.

"You know more than you think." His dark eyes held mine. "And we're going to piece it together before they make good on that threat."

I pulled the blanket tighter around myself. "I'm glad you're here. That I don't have to face this alone."

"You're not alone." His voice was firm. "Not as long as I'm around."

The words hung in the air between us, weighted with meaning beyond the current danger. Something had been starting to shift between us since the day we met. Neither of us acknowledged it directly, but it was there. A connection growing stronger with each shared moment.

That night, I lay on Lance's couch listening to the quiet sounds of the apartment. King's soft snoring, the puppies shifting in their makeshift bed, Lance's steady breathing from the bedroom. Despite the threats, despite the fear, I felt safer than I had in days.

Someone was after me. But they'd have to get through Lance first.

And somehow, I knew they wouldn't succeed.

Chapter Eight

I woke up on Lance's couch with Daisy sleeping on my chest, Bella curled against my legs, and Minnie wedged between the cushions and my hip. For a moment, I forgot where I was and why. Then the memory crashed back. The threatening note, the figure at the dog park, someone wanting me dead.

"Coffee's ready." Lance emerged from the kitchen, already dressed for the day in jeans and a dark blue Henley that made his eyes look almost black. He handed me a steaming mug.

"You're a lifesaver." I sat up carefully, trying not to disturb the puppy pile. "What time is it?"

"Seven thirty. Martinez called. He wants us to come to the station later this morning to go over everything again." Lance sat in the armchair with his own coffee, King settling at his feet. "But first, didn't you say you had maintenance requests to handle today?"

I groaned. "Yes. An air conditioning filter that needs to be changed, and Mr. Harrison in 115 reported a dripping faucet." I took a sip of coffee. Perfect, just like yesterday. "I should get back to my apartment and change."

"I'll walk you over."

"It's literally across the courtyard."

"I'll walk you over." His tone left no room for argument.

Thirty minutes later, showered and changed into clean jeans and a t-shirt that didn't smell like a garbage disposal, I gathered my toolbox and headed to Mrs. Wilson's apartment. Lance insisted on coming along, claiming he needed to learn more about the property's systems anyway.

Mrs. Wilson's air conditioning filter change was straightforward. Just pop off the vent cover, slide out the old filter, and slide in the new one. She offered us homemade dumplings, which I politely declined since I'd already had breakfast, but Lance accepted with genuine enthusiasm.

"Your aunt used to love my dumplings." Mrs. Wilson wrapped up half a dozen for Lance to take home. "She was a good woman. Always took care of us."

The comment made my chest tight. I was trying to fill some very big shoes.

Mr. Harrison's apartment was on the second floor, with a view overlooking the dog park and the lake beyond. I knocked three times before he answered, and when he did, he looked startled to see us.

"Oh. Ms. Waters. I wasn't expecting you so soon." Brian Harrison was in his mid-forties, thin and pale, like he didn't spend much time outdoors. His hair stuck up in odd directions, and he wore thick glasses that magnified his eyes. He blocked the doorway with his body, not inviting us in.

"You reported a dripping faucet?" I tried to peer past him into the apartment, but he shifted to block my view.

"Yes, but actually, I think I fixed it myself. Tightened the handle. No need for you to come in." He started to close the door.

Lance put his hand on the doorframe. "Mind if we check anyway? Sometimes those temporary fixes don't hold."

Brian's eyes darted between us nervously. "I really don't think…"

"It'll only take a minute." Something was off about his behavior. "I need to verify the repair for my records."

He hesitated, then reluctantly stepped back. "Fine. But please be quick. I'm very busy."

The apartment was dark despite the morning sun, with heavy curtains drawn over every window. As my eyes adjusted, I noticed equipment set up near the window facing the park. A large telescope on a tripod, several cameras with telephoto lenses, and what looked like audio recording equipment.

My heart rate spiked. This was the kind of setup someone would use for surveillance. For watching people.

Lance noticed it too. I felt the tension radiating from him as he moved closer to the equipment.

"The faucet's in the bathroom?" I did my best to keep my voice normal.

"Yes. Down the hall." Brian wrung his hands, his eyes fixed on Lance, who examined the telescope. "Please, don't touch that. It's expensive."

I went to the bathroom and turned on the faucet. It worked perfectly. No drip. When I returned to the living room, Lance was standing very still, his cop face on.

"That's quite a setup you have there," Lance said conversationally. "What are you watching?"

"I... it's nothing. Just a hobby." Brian's face flushed red. "The faucet's fine? Good. You can go now."

"Mr. Harrison," I said carefully, "have you been watching the dog park at night?"

His eyes went wide behind his glasses. "I have a right to look out my own window!"

"Of course you do," Lance agreed, his tone calm but firm. "But there's been a murder investigation, and someone with surveillance equipment pointed at the park might have seen something important."

"I didn't see anything!" Brian's voice rose and

grew panicked. "I wasn't watching people. I would never. I'm not some pervert."

"Then what are you watching?" I asked.

"I can't tell you. It's secret. Private." He backed toward the door, clearly wanting us to leave.

Lance pulled out his phone. "I'm going to have to call Detective Martinez about this."

"No. Please." Brian looked genuinely distressed now. "I'll show you, okay? Just don't call the police. I'm not doing anything wrong."

He rushed to a filing cabinet and pulled out a thick binder, thrusting it at me. I opened it to find detailed notes, sketches, and photographs. Not of people, but of birds. Owls, specifically. Pages and pages of observations about hunting patterns, flight paths, nesting behaviors.

"I'm documenting the great horned owl migration pattern through this area." His words tumbled out in a rush. "There's a mating pair that's been using the park for hunting. They're magnificent. But if anyone finds out and it gets publicized, people will flood the area to see them. It'll disrupt their patterns, stress them out. They might abandon the territory."

I looked at Lance, who flipped through the binder with a bemused expression.

"You're a birdwatcher," Lance said.

"Ornithologist, actually. Well, amateur. But serious about it." Brian pushed his glasses up his nose. "The owls hunt at night, which is why I have to observe after dark. And I need the telescope and cameras to document them without disturbing their natural behavior. That's why I've been keeping the curtains closed during the day. To maintain consistent light conditions for my night vision equipment."

"Have you been out to the park at night?" I asked. "Specifically, around the time Richard Thornton was killed?"

"No. I observe from here. I never go out there during active observation periods. That would defeat the entire purpose." He grabbed the binder back from Lance. "Please don't tell anyone about the owls. I'm submitting this documentation to the Audubon Society. It could be essential for understanding migration patterns in urban environments."

Lance and I exchanged glances. The man was clearly eccentric and secretive, but he wasn't a killer. He was just a passionate bird nerd trying to protect his owls.

"We won't tell anyone," I promised. "But Mr. Harrison, did you see anything unusual the night of the murder? Anyone near the park or on the trails?"

He thought for a moment, consulting a notebook. "Let me check my logs. I note any disturbances that might affect the owls' behavior." He flipped through pages of meticulous handwriting. "Here. The night of the twenty-third. I noticed unusual activity around 10:47 PM. Two people on the trail near the lake. They were arguing. I couldn't see faces. It was too dark, and I was focused on the owls, but I recorded it as a potential disruption."

My pulse quickened. "Two people arguing near where the body was found?"

"Could you tell anything about them?" Lance asked. "Height, build, gender?"

"One was definitely larger than the other. I remember thinking the smaller person seemed agitated—lots of arm movements. The larger person was more still." Brian squinted, trying to remember. "I'm sorry, I wasn't really paying attention. The owls were hunting, and that's much more interesting than whatever drama people were having."

Lance pulled out his phone. "I need you to tell this to Detective Martinez. And bring your logs."

Brian looked panicked again. "But the owls—"

"Are not going to be publicized by the police," Lance assured him. "This is a murder investigation. Your observations could be crucial."

After we left Brian's apartment, promising he'd call Martinez within the hour, Lance and I stood in the hallway looking at each other.

"A birdwatcher," I said.

"A birdwatcher," Lance confirmed.

And then he smiled. A real, genuine smile that transformed his entire face. The perpetual tension around his eyes eased, the hard line of his mouth softened, and suddenly I could see the man he must have been before the injury, before the forced leave, before whatever darkness had settled over him.

He took my breath away. He was absolutely gorgeous when he smiled.

"What?" His brow furrowed as his smile faded.

"Nothing. I just... you should smile more often." Heat flooded my cheeks. "You look less like you're about to arrest someone."

"Do I really look that intimidating?"

"Yes. Except when you're smiling. Then you look..." I trailed off, not quite ready to finish that sentence.

"Look what?" He stepped closer, and my heart did a little flip.

"Approachable. Nice." Handsome. Kissable. I kept those last thoughts to myself.

We started walking toward the stairs, our shoulders occasionally brushing. "I have to admit," Lance said, "I enjoyed that. The investigating, piecing together what was really happening. Even if it turned out to be owls instead of a killer."

"You were very thorough. Very detective-like." I glanced at him. "You're good at this. I can see why you miss it."

"I'd forgotten what it feels like. That rush when the pieces start fitting together." His expression turned more serious. "Thank you."

"For what?"

"For reminding me who I am. Who I was. Maybe who I can be again." He held the door open for me as we exited the building. "Working with you on this, helping you, investigating with you…it's the first time since the injury that I've felt like myself."

My throat tightened with emotion. "Lance—"

"I know it's not my case. I know I'm on leave and shouldn't even be involved. But Martinez is letting me help, and you…" He looked at me, something vulnerable in his expression. "You make me want to be better. To get back to where I was."

"You're already pretty great," I said softly.

We crossed the courtyard, heading toward the parking lot for our meeting with Martinez. King trotted ahead of us. I'd left my puppies safely in Lance's apartment with food and water.

"Do you think Brian's testimony will help?" I asked.

"Definitely. Two people arguing at the murder scene around the time of death? That's significant." Lance's mind was clearly working through the implications. "If we can figure out who those two people were, we might have our killer."

"Or at least a witness."

"Either way, it could be a break in the case." He pulled out his keys as we reached his truck. "And we found it together. Not bad for a property manager and a washed-up cop."

"You're not washed up," I protested. "You're on medical leave. There's a difference."

"Tell that to the brass." But he smiled again as he

said it, and I realized that maybe, just maybe, he was starting to believe he could come back from this.

At the police station, we sat across from Martinez's desk while Brian Harrison nervously recounted his observations from the night of the murder. Martinez listened intently, taking detailed notes.

"This is good," Martinez said when Brian finished. "Very good. The timeline matches what we suspected. Mr. Harrison, I'll need copies of your logs for that evening."

"Will you keep the owl information confidential?" Brian asked anxiously.

"The owls are not relevant to my investigation," Martinez assured him. "Your secret is safe."

After Brian left, promising to email his documentation, Martinez leaned back in his chair and studied us. "You two make a good team."

Lance and I glanced at each other.

"Crystal has good instincts," Lance said. "She noticed Harrison's odd behavior and didn't let it go."

"And Lance knows how to interview people without making them defensive," I added. "Brian would have clammed up completely if I'd been alone."

Martinez's expression was knowing. "Like I said. Good team. But…" He speared me with a sharp gaze. "You are not law enforcement. Nosing around could get you killed." He pulled out a file. "Based on Brian's testimony, we're looking at two people at the scene.

One smaller, agitated. One larger, calmer. That matches the evidence we found—the torn fabric suggests a struggle, and the coral lipstick on that coffee cup you photographed suggests a woman."

My eyes widened. "The coffee cup I found by the creek?"

"We sent someone to retrieve it based on your photos. Good eye, by the way." Martinez opened the file. "The lipstick is a high-end brand. Expensive. Same shade Victoria Thornton wears."

"But you said she had an alibi," I said. I remembered then the color she wore when she paid me a visit.

"She does. For most of the evening. But there's a two-hour window where she could have left the gala, driven here, and returned without being missed." Martinez looked between us. "I'm bringing her in for questioning this afternoon."

Lance sat forward. "You think she hired someone to kill her ex-husband?"

"I think she had motive. The divorce settlement wasn't as clean as she claims. Richard was contesting it, trying to prove she had hidden assets. If he'd won, she'd have owed him millions." Martinez closed the file. "And I think she's been lying about her relationship with him. They weren't as divorced as she pretends."

The pieces were starting to come together. Victoria's strange visit asking me to preserve the park. Was she fishing for information as to how much I knew? The threatening notes could be her trying to scare me away from the investigation.

"Be careful," Martinez warned. "If Victoria is behind this, she's already proven she's willing to kill. Those threats against you are real. I think you should both step back and stay low. The department is handling this."

As we left the station, Lance took my hand. The gesture felt natural, protective, and something more.

"We're going to figure this out," he said. "Together."

I squeezed his hand, feeling the strength and warmth of his grip. "Together," I agreed. Martinez hadn't ordered us to stop investigating, so we weren't breaking any laws, right?

And for the first time since finding Thornton's body, I felt like maybe everything would be okay because I wasn't facing this alone. I had Lance—brooding, protective, gradually-starting-to-smile-again Lance—by my side.

And somehow, that made all the difference.

Chapter Nine

Lance was gone when I woke the next morning, but had kindly left me a pot of fresh coffee on the kitchen counter along with a note in his neat handwriting: "Had to run some errands. Lock the door behind you. -L"

I smiled at the protective instruction, warmth spreading through my chest that had nothing to do with the coffee. Thankful that he lived on the ground floor, I opened the arcadia door and let the dogs, including King, out to do their business on his small patio while I sipped the brew that would help me function for the rest of the day.

King supervised the puppies with patient tolerance, his German Shepherd instincts making him a natural guardian. Minnie, Daisy, and Bella tumbled over each other in their enthusiasm to explore every corner of the small patio.

Morning routine done, I gathered up all four dogs,

left King food and water since Lance was out, and headed back to my own apartment. After settling my three dachshunds with breakfast, I grabbed a pooper scooper and a bag and marched to the courtyard to clean up after residents' dogs. Even with a sign that said to clean up after your pet, I spent the beginning of most days cleaning up after someone else's dog. Not to mention the stray cats who insisted on using the potted plants as litter boxes. Still, I preferred animals to most people.

The courtyard was relatively quiet this morning, just a few early risers heading to their cars for work. Mrs. Henderson waved from her balcony, and I waved back, making a mental note to check on her air conditioning system later this week.

"Hey, Ms. Waters?"

I turned as Brian Morrison rushed toward me, his telescope bag slung over his shoulder. He looked disheveled, like he hadn't slept much. "Good morning, Brian."

"I guess." He stopped and took a deep breath, his eyes darting around nervously. "I remembered something about the night Thornton died."

My heart rate picked up. "Really?" I leaned the scooper against a tree and gave him my full attention. "What do you remember?"

"I saw Mark Shuford last night as I was out walking. That's what jogged my memory." He pushed his glasses up his nose, a nervous gesture I was beginning to recognize. "I told you and Lance that I saw two people that night, but I really saw three. Only Shuford wasn't with the other two."

I wanted to ask him to get to the point. I had a full to-do list—the garbage disposal in 89 was acting up again, and someone had reported a leaking toilet in 156. But I really wanted to know what information he'd remembered. "Go on."

"Anyway, when I saw him last night, I asked him what he was doing at the park around 9:15 p.m. that night. He said he needed to clear his head. Claims he went toward the creek, not the park." Brian's face flushed with indignation. "That's a lie, Ms. Waters. I see clearly through my telescope or binoculars. I know which way he headed. He went straight toward where Thornton's body was found."

The implications hit me like a physical blow. Mark Shuford had been near the murder scene around the time of death. And he'd lied about it. "That's great information, Mr. Morrison. I'll pass it along to Detective Martinez."

"I already called him." Brian crossed his arms, looking as if he wanted me to argue about what he'd seen. "I'm only telling you because you seem so interested. Martinez is bringing Shuford in for questioning this afternoon."

"Thank you for telling me." I managed a smile despite my churning stomach. "This could be really important."

"I hope so. Thornton was a jerk, but nobody deserves to be murdered." He spun and marched away, his telescope bag bouncing against his hip.

I stared after him for a minute before tossing the bag of poo into the nearest trash can and returning to my apartment. My mind raced with possibilities. Mark Shuford, the restaurant owner facing financial ruin because of Thornton. Mark Shuford, who'd been heard threatening Thornton just days before the murder. Mark Shuford, who'd been at the scene around the time of death and lied about it.

It all pointed to him. But something nagged at me. It seemed almost too obvious.

I needed to focus on something else or I'd drive myself crazy theorizing. I decided to go through more of my aunt's paperwork. While she kept meticulous records, she also didn't seem to throw anything away. I'd found receipts dating back to the 1990s, ticket stubs from movies I'd never heard of, and enough doilies to cover every surface in a Victorian mansion.

When I opened a file containing medical records, I paused. My hands stilled on the papers as I read through doctors' notes and prescription records. Unbeknownst to me, my aunt suffered from vertigo and Meniere's disease. The records showed multiple visits to specialists, medications for dizziness and balance issues, even a note from her doctor warning her to be careful on stairs.

It seems as if her death was an accident after all.

I let the papers fall to the desktop as a new wave of grief washed over me. All this time, I'd had a nagging suspicion in the back of my mind that something was off about Aunt Mary Jane's fall. The timing, the fact that Thornton had wanted to buy Riverside Towers, the threats I'd been receiving. But the medical records painted a clear picture. A woman with severe balance issues had fallen down the stairs. It was tragic, but it was an accident. A bit of relief that she hadn't been murdered trickled through me.

Tears pricked my eyes. Accident or not, I missed her very much. I wished I'd visited more often, called more frequently, been a better niece. She'd left me everything, and I'd barely been part of her life these past few years.

I slipped the file into a box designated for storage. I might not want all her things cluttering up the apartment, but I wasn't quite ready to get rid of them yet either. They were all I had left of her.

Two hours later, home office in order, I decided to take the dogs for a walk down the hiking trail. I'd sat so long, my body thought rigor mortis had started to set in. My neck ached, my shoulders were tight, and I needed fresh air and sunshine to clear my head.

The afternoon felt warm but pleasant, with a light breeze that rustled the leaves overhead. Other walkers passed us on the trail. A jogger with earbuds, a couple holding hands, a woman with a golden retriever that made Minnie growl.

The crime scene tape no longer marked the spot where I'd discovered Thornton's body, but I tried to steer the dogs away from that spot anyway. Three determined dachshunds were not easy to drag away from a place they wanted to investigate. Their noses were locked onto some scent, and they pulled against their leashes with surprising strength for such small dogs.

"Minnie!" Ugh. She'd slipped free of her halter and into the bushes before I could stop her. Daisy and Bella started whining and yipping like I was hurting them. "Hush, girls. Minnie, get back here."

I shoved aside some low-hanging branches to find Minnie digging at the spot Thornton had laid. The earth was loose here, disturbed by the police investigation and not yet fully settled. Soon, the other two dogs joined in, and dirt went flying, striking my face and getting stuck in my hair.

"Stop it! All of you." I tried to sound authoritative, but I might as well have been talking to a tree.

There couldn't be anything left to find. The police would've already dug up any evidence left behind, right? Martinez and his team had been thorough. They'd photographed everything, collected samples, searched the entire area.

I put Minnie's halter back on her, not easy to do when she wanted to dig. More like fighting an alligator. She twisted and squirmed, her little paws scrabbling at my hands. "Enough." I dragged the dogs a few feet away, then peered into the six-inch deep hole they'd created, only to find the bones of a small rodent. Gross.

Well, that explained their interest. Nothing sinister, just the remains of some poor mouse or mole that had met its end here long before Thornton had.

My three fur babies behaved the rest of the way home, their digging urge satisfied. I spotted Lance in the courtyard talking to one of the residents and tossed him a wave. "Coffee later?"

He grinned and nodded, leaving me feeling like a girl with a teenage crush. My stomach did that annoying flip thing it had been doing lately whenever he smiled at me.

I spent the rest of the afternoon handling maintenance requests and trying not to think about Mark Shuford being questioned by Martinez. Was he the killer? Had I been living in the same complex as a murderer this whole time?

By the time Lance knocked on my door at seven that night, I'd worked myself into a state of nervous energy. I'd showered and changed into comfortable clothes, yoga pants and an oversized sweatshirt, and had coffee already brewing.

"You look tired," I said as I let him in. And he did. The lines around his eyes were deeper, and he moved with a heaviness that suggested exhaustion.

"Long day." He sank into one of my kitchen chairs with a grateful sigh. "I've been helping Martinez unofficially. Reviewing evidence, offering insights. It feels good to be useful again."

I poured us both coffee and sat across from him at the small kitchen table. The apartment was quiet except for the soft snoring of three sleeping dachshunds piled on the couch. "Did you hear about Brian Morrison's statement? About seeing Mark Shuford near the park?"

"I did." Lance wrapped his hands around his mug, the steam rising between us. "Martinez brought Shuford in for questioning this afternoon. He admits he went for a walk to 'clear his head' but claims he went toward the river, not the park."

"But Brian says that's a lie."

"Brian's testimony is solid. He keeps detailed logs, has time-stamped photos from his owl observations. Shuford was definitely near the park around 9:15 PM." Lance took a sip of coffee. "The question is…why is he lying about it?"

I leaned forward, my elbows on the table. "Do you think he killed Thornton?"

Lance was quiet for a long moment, his cop face firmly in place. "The evidence is circumstantial but compelling. Motive—Thornton was destroying his business. Opportunity—he was at the scene around the time of death. Means—the murder weapon was a rock from the park, something anyone could have picked up."

"But?" I heard the hesitation in his voice.

"But murder investigations aren't always logical.

Sometimes the obvious suspect is the right one. Sometimes they're not." He met my eyes across the table. "Martinez is building a case. They're searching Shuford's home and restaurant for evidence. Clothing that might match the torn fabric, shoes that match the footprints. If they find a connection, he'll be arrested."

"You don't sound convinced."

"I'm not unconvinced either." Lance smiled slightly. "I've learned not to jump to conclusions. Evidence tells the story, not my gut instinct."

"What does Martinez think about all this? Me being involved, I mean." I wrapped my hands around my own mug, seeking warmth. "I keep stumbling into evidence, getting threats, asking questions."

"He's concerned." Lance's expression turned serious. "He warned me today that civilian interference can complicate investigations. But he also acknowledged that you've provided valuable information. The coffee cup, Brian's odd behavior, Victoria's strange visit…all of it has been useful."

"I'm not trying to interfere." I crossed my arms. "I'm just trying to stay alive and figure out what's happening on my own property."

"I know." He wiggled his fingers as a sign to get me to relax. When I reached for my mug, his hand covered mine on the table, warm and reassuring. "And I told Martinez that. But Crystal, you need to be careful. If Shuford is the killer and he thinks you know something or saw something that could incriminate him, you're in danger."

A chill ran down my spine despite the warm coffee. "The threats."

"Exactly. Someone is trying to scare you off. Whether it's Shuford or someone else, they see you as a problem." His thumb brushed across my knuckles, a gesture that was becoming familiar and far too easy to get used to. "That's why I want you to stay vigilant. Keep your doors locked. Don't go anywhere alone. And if anything, anything at all, seems off, you call me immediately."

"I will." I turned my hand over so our palms pressed together. "Thank you. For everything. For protecting me, for helping me understand all this, for just...being here."

"There's nowhere else I'd rather be." His dark eyes held mine, and something passed between us. An acknowledgment of feelings neither of us was quite ready to name. "You've reminded me who I used to be. Who I want to be again."

"You're already there," I whispered. "The injury doesn't define you."

"Sometimes it feels like it does." His voice was rough with emotion. "But with you, working on this, helping you...I feel like myself again. Like I'm more than just a broken cop waiting for medical clearance."

We sat in silence for a while, hands clasped across the table, the only sound the ticking of Aunt Mary Jane's brass clock and the occasional snore from the couch.

"Do you think we'll catch them?" I finally asked. "Whoever killed Thornton?"

"Yes." No hesitation. "Martinez is good at his job. And now that Shuford is a prime suspect, it's only a matter of time before we find the evidence we need."

"And if it's not him?"

"Then we keep looking." Lance squeezed my hand. "Until you're safe. Until justice is served. We don't stop."

That "we" made my heart stutter. We. A team. Partners.

Maybe something more.

When Lance finally left around ten, I locked the door behind him as instructed and checked all the windows. He'd wanted me to stay with him again, but three dogs were a well-enough security system. I settled on the couch with my sleeping puppies, too wired to go to bed, my mind replaying the conversation.

Shuford was the prime suspect. The evidence pointed to him. But something about all of this still didn't sit right with me.

I thought about Victoria Thornton's strange visit, her insistence that Richard had been a good man who loved the park. About Linda's gossip about Janet Hooper and her euthanized dog. About Jack Bradley and his environmental activism.

And I thought about the coffee cup with coral lipstick. Victoria's shade.

Tomorrow, I'd talk to Lance about it. Tomorrow, we'd figure out what piece of the puzzle was still missing.

But tonight, I'd let myself feel safe, warmed by coffee and conversation and the memory of Lance's hand in mine.

Chapter Ten

I was refilling the coffee station in the community room when Linda burst through the door, practically vibrating with gossip energy.

"You'll never guess what I just found out," she announced, not bothering with pleasantries.

I sighed and set down the coffee canister. "Good morning to you too, Linda."

"Yes, yes, good morning. But seriously, Crystal, this is huge." She glanced around to make sure we were alone, then lowered her voice to what she probably thought was a whisper. "Emma Patterson, you know, the dog walker who thinks she's better than everyone else and trying to steal my business, was having an affair with Richard Thornton!"

My hand stilled on the coffee maker. "What?"

"I know!" Linda's eyes gleamed with the thrill of sharing explosive information. "My friend Shelly, she does grooming at Pampered Paws, she saw them together at that fancy restaurant downtown, Ember & Oak, about six months ago. Very cozy, very intimate. And get this: the affair ended badly about three months ago."

"How does Shelly know it ended badly?"

"Because Emma came into the grooming salon crying her eyes out, saying she'd been used and discarded like garbage. Shelly put two and two together." Linda leaned against the counter, clearly settling in for a long gossip session. "Apparently, Richard promised to leave Victoria for her, then broke it off out of nowhere and threatened to ruin Emma's business if she told anyone about the affair."

My mind raced. Emma Patterson had motive—betrayal, humiliation, the threat to her livelihood. "Does Martinez know about this?"

Linda's face fell slightly. "I don't know. I just found out this morning. You should tell him, though. You're much more involved in the investigation than I am."

"I'm not involved in the investigation," I protested automatically, even though we both knew it was a lie at this point. "But yes, I'll make sure Martinez knows."

After Linda left, reluctantly, after I promised to tell her any updates, I pulled out my phone and called Lance. He answered on the second ring.

"Miss me already?" I could hear the smile in his voice.

I gave a nervous giggle. "But I just got some

interesting information about Emma Patterson. You know, the dog walker?"

"Linda's rival. I've seen her at the park." His tone shifted to professional. "What about her?"

I relayed everything Linda had told me, and Lance was quiet for a moment.

"That's a solid motive," he finally said. "But we need to verify it before going to Martinez. Anonymous gossip isn't evidence."

"So, what do we do?"

"We talk to Emma. Informally. You're the property manager, you have a legitimate reason to speak to residents about the ongoing investigation." I could almost see him thinking through the approach. "I'll come with you as...moral support."

"Backup, you mean."

"That too."

An hour later, Lance and I stood outside Emma Patterson's door in building C. She lived in apartment 178, a one-bedroom unit with a view of the dog park. Through the door, I heard multiple dogs barking.

"Ready?" Lance asked quietly.

I nodded and knocked.

The barking intensified, followed by Emma's voice commanding the dogs to be quiet. When she opened the door, she looked harried and exhausted. Her blonde hair was pulled back in a messy ponytail, and she wore yoga pants and a t-shirt that advertised her dog walking business: "Patterson's Paws—Professional

Pet Care."

"Ms. Waters." Her eyes flicked to Lance with obvious interest. "And Mr. Hendricks. What can I do for you?"

"May we come in?" I asked, trying to sound official but friendly. "I'm following up with residents who use the dog park regularly. With the ongoing investigation, I want to make sure everyone feels safe."

She hesitated, then stepped back. "Of course. Excuse the mess. I'm watching six dogs today."

The apartment was clean despite the chaos of multiple dogs. Three were in crates, sleeping, while two played tug-of-war with a rope toy. A nervous-looking Chihuahua hid under the couch. The living room had been set up as a mini dog daycare, with water bowls, toys, and training pads.

"Impressive operation," Lance said, his tone neutral and professional.

"Thank you. I take my business seriously." Emma gestured to the couch, moving the rope toy so we could sit. "Can I get you anything? Water? Coffee?"

"We're fine, thank you." I sat, and Lance settled beside me, close enough that our shoulders touched. The contact was reassuring. "I wanted to ask about the night Richard Thornton was killed. I understand you're a regular at the dog park?"

Emma's expression shuttered immediately. "Why are you asking? Shouldn't the police be handling this?"

"They are," Lance said smoothly. "But Ms.

Waters is concerned about her residents' safety. The more information we can gather, the better."

"We?" Emma's eyes narrowed. "Are you two working together on this?"

"Mr. Hendricks has been helping me with property maintenance." Which was technically true. "And he's been kind enough to accompany me during these follow-up visits."

Emma studied us for a long moment, then seemed to relax slightly. "Fine. Yes, I was at the park that night. I walk dogs every evening around seven thirty. It's part of my routine."

"Did you see anything unusual?" I asked.

"No. It was a normal evening. I walked my clients' dogs, cleaned up after them, and went home." Her answers were too practiced, too smooth.

Lance leaned forward, his elbows on his knees. "What time did you leave the park?"

"Around eight. Maybe a little before." She crossed her arms. "Why?"

"The medical examiner places the time of death between nine PM and midnight," Lance said. "Did you return to the park after eight?"

"No." The word came out too quickly. "I went home."

"Can anyone verify that?" I tried to match Lance's calm, professional tone.

"I live alone. So, no." Emma stood abruptly. "Look, I don't know what this is really about, but I've told you everything I know. I was at the park, I left before eight, I didn't see anything suspicious. Is there anything else?"

Lance stood as well, and I followed. "Just one more thing," he said casually. "Did you know Richard Thornton personally?"

The color drained from Emma's face. "What? No. I mean, I knew who he was. Everyone did. He was trying to destroy the park."

"That's not what I asked." Lance's voice remained gentle but firm. "Did you know him personally?"

Emma's hands clenched into fists at her sides. "I think you should leave."

"Emma," I said softly, "if there's something you need to tell us, now's the time. The police are going to find out eventually. It's better if it comes from you."

For a moment, I thought she would slam the door in our faces. Then her shoulders sagged, and tears welled in her eyes. "Fine. Yes. I knew Richard." She sank back onto the couch, and the Chihuahua emerged from under it to jump into her lap. "We had an affair. It started about nine months ago and ended three months ago."

Lance and I exchanged glances. Linda's gossip had been accurate.

"What happened?" I sat beside her.

"He pursued me. Came to the dog park almost every day, struck up conversations, asked me to dinner." Emma's voice was bitter. "He said Victoria was cold, that their marriage was over in everything but name. He said he was going to leave her, that we'd be together."

"But he didn't leave her," Lance said.

"No. Three months ago, he broke it off with me. Said it was getting too complicated, that Victoria was suspicious. He said we needed to stop seeing each other." Emma wiped her eyes with the back of her hand. "When I got upset, when I said I'd tell Victoria everything, he threatened me. Said he'd ruin my business, spread rumors that I was neglectful with the dogs, get me blacklisted from every pet sitting service in the county."

"That must have made you very angry," I said carefully.

"Of course I was angry! I loved him. I believed him when he said he loved me too." Emma's tears flowed freely now. "But I didn't kill him. I swear I didn't."

"You said you left the park at eight," Lance said. "Are you sure about that time?"

Emma hesitated. "Maybe it was a little later. Eight fifteen? I wasn't really paying attention to the time."

"Emma, the police found a piece of torn fabric at the crime scene. Expensive fabric, like from a designer jacket." Lance pulled out his phone and showed her a photo Martinez had shared with him. "Do you recognize this?"

Emma's face went white. "I... that looks like my

jacket. The burgundy one with the gold buttons."

"Where is that jacket now?" I asked.

"I don't know. I haven't seen it in a while." Her words tumbled out in a rush. "It might be in my closet, or maybe I left it at a client's house, or—"

"Emma." Lance's voice was firm but not unkind. "You need to talk to Detective Martinez. Today. Tell him everything you just told us."

"But he'll think I did it! I was there, I had a motive, and now my jacket—" She broke off, her breathing coming in short gasps.

"If you didn't kill Richard, the truth will come out," I said. "But lying or hiding information only makes you look guilty."

Emma buried her face in her hands, the Chihuahua licking her fingers anxiously. "I didn't kill him. I was angry, yes. Hurt and betrayed and humiliated. But I didn't kill him."

"Then help us find who did," Lance said. "Tell Martinez about the affair. Let him examine your jacket. If you're innocent, the evidence will prove it."

After extracting Emma's promise to contact Martinez within the hour, Lance and I left her apartment and walked to the parking lot in silence.

"Well," I finally said, "that was intense."

"Good work in there." Lance's hand found mine, our fingers intertwining naturally. "You kept her talking, asked the right questions, showed empathy. You're a natural at this."

Heat rose to my cheeks. "I just followed your lead. You knew exactly how to approach her, when to push and when to back off."

"We make a good team." He stopped beside his truck, turning to face me. "It felt... natural. Working with you."

"It did, didn't it?" I suddenly became very aware of how close we were standing. "Like we've been doing this together for years instead of days."

His free hand came up to tuck a strand of hair behind my ear, his fingers lingering on my cheek. "Crystal—"

My phone rang, shattering the moment. I pulled it out reluctantly to see Martinez's name on the screen. "It's the detective."

Lance stepped back, giving me space, but didn't release my hand.

"Hello?"

"Ms. Waters, I need you to come down to the station. Emma Patterson just called me in tears saying you and Lance Hendricks ambushed her in her apartment." Martinez's voice was controlled but I could hear the frustration underneath. "Care to explain?"

I grimaced. "We were following up on information that came to me through a resident. I wanted to verify it before wasting your time."

"That's not your job. That's my job. That's what police do." He sighed heavily. "Look, I appreciate that you've provided valuable information, and I know

Lance has experience with investigations. But you can't just go around interrogating suspects. It compromises the investigation and potentially puts you in danger."

"I'm sorry. I didn't think—"

"That's right. You didn't think." Martinez's tone softened slightly. "But since you did it, and since Emma is coming in to give a statement, I need to know exactly what was said. Both of you. Station. One hour." He hung up before I could respond.

"We're in trouble," I told Lance.

"Worth it, though." He grinned, apparently unconcerned about Martinez's irritation. "Emma's coming in, she's going to tell the truth, and we've added another suspect to the list."

"Another suspect who has motive, opportunity, and physical evidence connecting her to the crime scene," I pointed out. "Between Mark Shuford and Emma Patterson, Martinez has his hands full."

"Maybe that's a good thing. Multiple suspects means the investigation is progressing." Lance opened his truck door. "Come on. Let's go face the music."

As we drove to the station, I found myself studying Lance's profile. The strong line of his jaw, the concentration in his dark eyes, the hint of a smile playing at his lips despite the trouble we were in.

Working with him felt right. Natural. Like we were two halves of a whole, complementing each other's strengths and covering each other's weaknesses.

It was terrifying and exhilarating at the same time.

At the station, Martinez made us sit in separate rooms and give our statements independently. When I was finally released an hour later, Lance waited for me in the lobby, leaning against the wall with his arms crossed.

"Lecture over?" he asked.

"Thoroughly lectured." I walked toward him, grateful to see a friendly face. "You?"

"Martinez threatened to have me arrested for obstruction if I interfere with the investigation again as a civilian." Lance pushed off the wall and fell into step beside me. "Then he thanked me for getting Emma to come forward and asked if I'd consult on the case officially."

My eyes widened. "Really?"

"Really. Turns out he's been understaffed and could use someone with my experience." Lance held the door open for me as we exited the building. "It would give me something to do while I'm on medical leave. And it would be legitimate this time."

"That's wonderful!" I threw my arms around him in an impulsive hug.

He stiffened for just a moment, then his arms came around me, solid and warm. We stood there in the parking lot, holding each other, neither of us wanting to let go.

"Crystal," he murmured against my hair.

"Hmm?"

"I really like working with you. And not just

because of the case."

My heart stuttered. "I really like working with you too. And not just because you fix my broken washing machines."

He laughed, the sound rumbling through his chest where I pressed against him. "We should probably talk about this. About us."

"Probably," I agreed. But neither of us moved.

Eventually, we had to separate. We had lives to get back to—maintenance requests, dog walking, a murder investigation. But something had shifted between us today. Something important.

As Lance drove me back to Riverside Towers, I couldn't help but smile. Yes, there was a killer out there. Yes, I'd been threatened and was potentially in danger. Yes, Martinez was irritated with me for playing amateur detective.

But I'd found something I wasn't looking for in the middle of all this chaos. Someone I wasn't looking for.

And that made all the danger almost worth it.

Almost.

Chapter Eleven

I was having such a good day until everything went sideways.

The morning had been unusually productive—I'd fixed a leaky faucet without flooding anything, answered tenant emails without getting sidetracked, and even managed to box up three more containers of Aunt Mary Jane's porcelain figurines. Daisy and Bella had been angels during their training session, actually sitting on command for a full three seconds.

So naturally, I decided to reward everyone with a trip to the dog park.

Lance met me at the gate, King trotting beside him with his usual dignified air. My three dachshunds immediately started yapping excitedly, their tails wagging so hard their entire back ends shook.

"Good afternoon." Lance's eyes crinkled with that smile I'd come to look forward to seeing. He'd been officially consulting with Martinez for two days now, and the purpose it gave him was obvious. He stood taller, moved with more confidence, seemed more like the man he was meant to be.

"Afternoon." I fumbled with the latch on the small dog enclosure, juggling three leashes while trying to open the gate. "How's the case going?"

"Making progress. Martinez is running down leads on both Emma and Mark." He reached over to help with the gate. "Emma's jacket is a match for the torn fabric. The lab confirmed it this morning."

My stomach dropped. "So, she's—"

"A person of interest. Not arrested yet. They still need more evidence." Lance held the gate open while I herded my three dogs inside. "Her timeline is shaky, and she has motive, but no direct evidence placing her at the actual murder."

I unclipped the leashes, and predictably, Minnie immediately pressed against my leg while Daisy and Clarabelle bounded off to sniff every corner of the enclosure. King, ever patient, lay down near Lance's feet.

"What about Mark Shuford?" I sat on one of the weathered benches.

Lance settled beside me, close enough that our shoulders touched. "Still insisting he went to the creek, not the park. But his alibi doesn't hold up. We're waiting on forensics from his clothing."

We sat in comfortable silence for a few minutes, watching the dogs. A few other owners were scattered around the park with their pets, but the small dog section was relatively empty. Just us and our four troublemakers.

That's when I noticed the man.

He was standing near the entrance to the small dog enclosure, about twenty feet away, wearing a dark hoodie despite the warm afternoon. Something about his posture—the way he kept glancing at us, then away—set off alarm bells.

"Lance," I said quietly.

"I see him." Lance's voice was calm but alert. "Stay here."

He stood and started walking toward the gate, King immediately at attention beside him. The man in the hoodie noticed the approach and lunged forward, yanking open the gate to the small-dog enclosure.

"Hey!" Lance broke into a run, but the man was already sprinting toward the parking lot.

And Minnie, my timid, anxious, never-leaves-my-side Minnie, bolted through the open gate like her tail was on fire.

"Minnie!" I screamed, jumping to my feet. My heart stopped as I watched my baby disappear into the wooded area beyond the park. "Minnie, come back!"

Daisy and Bella charged toward the open gate, but I managed to scoop them up before they could follow. Lance had already abandoned his pursuit of the hoodie man and ran toward the woods where Minnie had vanished.

"Crystal, get the puppies secure and call Martinez!" he shouted over his shoulder. "Tell him what happened. Then meet me at the trailhead."

I stood frozen for a precious few seconds, my mind refusing to process what had just happened. Someone had deliberately opened the gate. Someone had tried to—what? Scare me? Hurt Minnie? Lure me into the woods?

None of that mattered right now. All that mattered was finding Minnie.

I rushed to my apartment, barely managing to unlock the door with my shaking hands, and deposited the two puppies inside with food and water. Then I called Martinez as I ran back outside.

"Someone opened the dog park gate," I said breathlessly when he answered. "A man in a hoodie. Minnie ran into the woods. Lance went after her."

"Are you safe?" Martinez's voice was sharp.

"I'm heading to the trailhead now. Lance said to meet him there."

"Crystal, no. Go back inside and lock your door. This could be a trap."

"My dog is out there!" Tears burned my eyes. "I'm not leaving her."

Martinez swore. "Fine. I'm on my way. Stay in open areas. Do not go into the woods alone. Wait for backup."

But I was already at the trailhead, where Lance and King were examining the ground. King's nose was to the dirt, his tail straight out in tracking mode.

"Anything?" I tried to keep the panic out of my voice.

"King's got her scent. She went this way." Lance pointed down the trail that led toward the lake. Toward where we'd found Thornton's body. "Stay close to me."

We moved quickly but carefully, King leading the way with his nose down. Lance kept one hand on my elbow, guiding me around roots and rocks I was too distracted to notice.

"Minnie!" I called out every few seconds. "Minnie, baby, come here!"

Nothing. Just the rustle of leaves and the distant sound of water.

"She's scared." My voice broke. "She's never been alone in the woods. What if she gets hurt? What if there are coyotes or—"

"King will find her." Lance's voice was firm, confident. "He's trained for this. We're going to find her, Crystal."

We'd been searching for maybe ten minutes, though it felt like hours, when King's ears perked up, and he let out a single sharp bark. Then he took off running down a narrow side trail I hadn't even noticed.

"King!" Lance called, but the German Shepherd was already crashing through the underbrush.

We followed, branches whipping at our faces and arms. My lungs burned, and my legs ached, but I didn't slow down. I couldn't.

And then I heard it. The most beautiful sound in the world.

Minnie's bark. High-pitched, anxious, but definitely her.

We burst into a small clearing, and there she was, digging frantically at the base of a large oak tree. King stood beside her, his tail wagging, as if to say, "I found her, now come get her."

"Minnie!" I dropped to my knees, and she immediately abandoned her digging to launch herself into my arms. I held her tight, tears streaming down my face as she licked every inch of my face she could reach. "Don't you ever do that to me again. Never, never, never."

Lance crouched beside us, his hand on my shoulder. "She's okay. You're both okay."

I nodded, unable to speak past the lump in my throat. For a moment, I just held my dog and let the relief wash over me.

Then I noticed where we were.

This clearing was less than fifty feet from where Thornton's body had been found. And Minnie had been digging. Just like she'd dug before, when she'd found the rodent bones.

"Lance," I said slowly. "Look at what she was digging."

He followed my gaze to the disturbed earth at the base of the oak tree. King, apparently deciding his work was done, had settled into a dignified sit nearby.

Lance pulled a small flashlight from his pocket; of course, he carried a flashlight, and examined the hole Minnie had created. His expression changed immediately.

"Don't touch anything." He pulled out his phone and started taking photos. "Crystal, I need you to step back with Minnie."

"What is it?"

"Evidence." He used a stick to carefully move some dirt aside, and I caught a glimpse of dark leather. "Looks like a wallet."

My heart pounded as Lance carefully extracted the wallet using the stick and a tissue from his pocket, making sure not to contaminate it with his fingerprints. It was expensive leather, water-damaged but still intact.

He opened it carefully. Inside were several bills—hundred-dollar bills, to be exact. A quick count revealed at least $5,000 in cash.

"Why would someone bury this much cash?" I whispered.

"Blackmail payment, maybe. Or a payoff." Lance photographed everything, his movements methodical and professional. Then he pulled out what looked like a folded piece of paper tucked behind the bills.

Using the tissue to handle it, he carefully unfolded the paper. Even from where I stood, I could see the block letters written in black marker:

"YOU KNOW WHAT YOU DID. THIS IS YOUR LAST WARNING."

The handwriting was deliberately disguised, the letters angular and unnatural, but the message was clear. Someone had been threatening Richard Thornton.

"Is this..." I trailed off, my mind trying to make sense of it.

"A threatening letter." Lance photographed it from multiple angles. "And if it was buried here, near the crime scene, the killer might have planted it. Or Thornton buried it himself before he died."

"Or someone else buried it, someone who knew what happened." I clutched Minnie tighter. "Lance, that man in the hoodie. He deliberately let Minnie out. Was this whole thing a setup? To get me to find this?"

Lance's expression darkened. "Or to get you into the woods alone. Away from witnesses." He pulled out his phone again. "Martinez is going to want to see this immediately. And we need to get you back to the complex. Now."

"But—"

"No arguments." His voice was firm. "Someone deliberately targeted your dog to lure you here. Whether it was to have you find this evidence or to have you vulnerable in the woods, either way, you're not safe."

He was right. I knew he was right. But the implication made my blood run cold. Someone was watching me. Tracking my movements. They knew which dog was mine, knew I'd panic and run into the woods after her.

The walk back to the trailhead felt twice as long, despite Lance setting a brisk pace. He kept me close, one hand on my arm, his eyes constantly scanning the trees around us. King walked point, alert and protective. Minnie trembled in my arms, but I wasn't about to put her down.

We were almost back to the main path when Lance suddenly stopped, his hand tightening on my arm.

"What—" I started, but he held up a finger for silence.

For several long seconds, we stood frozen, listening. I heard it then. The snap of a branch, the rustle of leaves that wasn't from the wind.

Someone was in the woods with us.

Lance's other hand went to his belt, where I noticed for the first time he was carrying his service weapon. King's hackles rose, and he positioned himself between us and the sound.

"Police! Identify yourself." Lance's voice rang out with authority.

The rustling stopped. Then, more movement, but this time, moving away from us. Running.

"Go," Lance commanded. "Straight to the trailhead. Don't stop."

We ran. I held Minnie against my chest with both arms, focusing on not tripping over roots or rocks. Behind us, I could hear Lance and King keeping pace a few feet behind me, their presence the only thing keeping me from complete panic.

We burst out of the woods to find Martinez and two uniformed officers waiting at the trailhead, hands on their weapons.

"Crystal!" Martinez lowered his gun. "Are you hurt?"

"No. But someone was following us. Lance heard them." I gasped for breath, my heart hammering against my ribs.

Lance emerged from the woods seconds later, King at his side. "Whoever it was ran north, toward the access road. They'll be long gone by now."

Martinez gestured to one of the officers. "Check it out anyway. And I want this entire area secured." He turned to Lance. "What happened?"

Lance relayed everything—the man in the hoodie, Minnie's escape, the wallet, and the threatening letter we'd found. Martinez's expression grew darker with each detail.

"You photographed everything?" he asked.

"Yes. And I left it exactly where we found it for your team to process properly." Lance pulled up the photos on his phone, showing them to Martinez.

"Good work." Martinez studied the images, his jaw tight. "This changes things. That handwriting is disguised, but our analysts might be able to determine who wrote it. And $5,000 in cash suggests payment for something. Blackmail, hiring a hitman, payoff for keeping quiet."

"Or Thornton was paying someone off, and they killed him anyway," I said quietly.

The three of them looked at me.

"It's possible," Martinez admitted. "We'll run down every angle." He focused on me. "Ms. Waters, I need you to go home, lock your doors, and stay inside for the rest of the day. Someone deliberately targeted you and your dog. This isn't a game anymore."

"It never was a game." My voice shook.

"Come on." Lance's hand found mine. "I'll walk you back."

Martinez didn't object, just nodded and turned to coordinate with his officers.

The walk back to Riverside Towers was quiet. I couldn't stop shaking, adrenaline still flooding my system. Minnie had stopped trembling but refused to let me put her down.

When we reached my apartment, Lance did a full sweep, checking closets, under the bed, behind the shower curtain, before declaring it safe.

"Thank you," I said when he finished. "For everything. For finding Minnie, for keeping me safe, for—"

I didn't get to finish. Lance pulled me into his arms, carefully, because I was still holding Minnie, and held me close. One hand cradled the back of my head, the other wrapped around my waist.

"I was terrified," he murmured against my hair. "When I saw Minnie run into the woods, when I realized someone had deliberately let her out, when I heard that branch snap behind us. I've never been so scared in my life."

I buried my face against his chest, breathing in the scent of him—soap and coffee and something uniquely Lance. "Me too."

We stood there for several long moments, just holding each other. His heart beat steady and strong beneath my ear. His arms felt safe, solid, like nothing could hurt me as long as I was in them.

Then, he released me and stepped back. His face flushed, and he cleared his throat.

"I should... I should go. Let you rest." He wouldn't quite meet my eyes. "Keep your door locked. Call me if you need anything. Anything at all."

"Lance—"

"I'll check on you later." He was already backing toward the door. "Get some rest, Crystal."

And then he was gone, leaving me standing in my living room with Minnie in my arms and my heart doing complicated things in my chest.

The hug had lasted maybe thirty seconds. But the feeling of his arms around me, the way he'd held me like I was precious and fragile and worth protecting…that lingered.

I set Minnie down and sank onto the couch, my mind replaying the afternoon. The deliberate sabotage at the dog park. The wallet with its threatening letter. Someone following us in the woods. And Lance, pulling me close in a moment of raw emotion before embarrassment made him retreat.

We hadn't talked about what was happening between us. We kept dancing around it, sharing meaningful looks and casual touches and moments of connection that felt like more than friendship.

But that hug, brief and spontaneous and immediately regretted, that had meant something.

I just wasn't sure what yet.

My phone buzzed with a text from Lance: "Door locked?"

I smiled despite everything. "Yes. Triple-checked."

"Good. Sleep with your phone nearby. And Crystal?"

"Yeah?"

"I meant what I said. Call me if you need anything. I don't care what time it is."

I stared at the message for a long moment before typing: "Thank you for finding Minnie. And for being there."

"Always."

That single word made my chest tight with emotion I wasn't ready to name.

I gathered my three dogs around me on the couch, needing their warm, solid presence. Somewhere out there was a killer who'd threatened me, lured my dog into the woods, and buried evidence near a crime scene.

But I also had Lance, protective, caring,

gradually-opening-up Lance, who'd searched the woods for my dog and held me like I mattered.

Tomorrow, we'd figure out what the wallet and letter meant. Tomorrow, Martinez would analyze the evidence and maybe catch a killer.

Tonight, I'd let myself feel safe in the memory of Lance's arms around me and the knowledge that he was just across the courtyard if I needed him.

It would have to be enough.

Chapter Twelve

I stared at yet another overflowing toilet. To be honest, I'd rather be covered with slime and gross toilet water than be threatened by a killer.

"What's down there?" The frazzled young mother in apartment 114 shrugged. "I'm guessing either an action figure or a toy car. My son likes his toys to go scuba diving." She tossed the three-year-old an exasperated look. "My husband usually fixes it, but he's away on vacation."

After several unsuccessful attempts with the plunger, I sent Lance a text, asking him to squeeze number 114 into his schedule, and then moved on to the next item on my to-do list. A smoke detector that wouldn't stop beeping. An easy fix. I replaced the battery and continued working down my list, taking the occasional break to let the dogs roam the courtyard while I ate a granola bar.

I started to feel more confident in my ability to

run Riverside Towers…for the most part. Removing toilets to clear them of toys was out of my experience.

"Ah!" The sprinklers came on, sending the dogs and me running. I'd been so wrapped up in my accomplishments, I'd forgotten the time. My feet slipped on a patch of wet leaves. Before I knew what was happening, I lay flat on my back staring at the sky while three dachshunds licked my face.

Linda laughed as two large mixed-breed dogs tugged her down the sidewalk. "See you later!"

I waved. If she wasn't a suspect in Thornton's death, I could see us being friends. I could use a friend to talk over girl stuff with. After lying there for a few minutes to catch my breath, I pushed to my feet and headed back to my apartment to change.

The door was closed, but not quite latched. Just slightly ajar, maybe an inch, like someone had pulled it shut but hadn't waited for the lock to click. My hand froze on the handle as my brain tried to process what I was seeing.

I always locked my door. Always. Triple-checked it, especially after the threats. And I definitely hadn't left it open this morning.

My phone was in my hand, and Lance's number dialed before I'd consciously decided to call him.

"Hey," he answered, warmth in his voice. "What's up?"

"My door is open." My voice came out steadier than I expected. "I locked it when I left. I know I did."

"Don't go inside." His tone shifted immediately to cop-sharp. "Do you hear me, Crystal? Do not go in that apartment. Where are you now?"

"Standing in the hallway. Outside the door."

"Stay there. I'm calling Martinez, and I'll be there in two minutes. Do not go inside."

He hung up, and I stood frozen in the hallway, staring at that barely open door. Part of me wanted to push it open, to see what damage had been done. The larger part of me, the part that had learned to listen to Lance's professional instincts, kept me rooted in place.

True to his word, Lance appeared at the end of the hallway ninety seconds later, King at his side. He had his service weapon drawn, held low and ready. "Get behind me."

I obeyed without argument, pressing my back against the wall while Lance approached the door. He used his foot to push it open wider, then moved inside with King, both of them alert and professional.

"Clear," he called out after a minute. "But…you need to prepare yourself."

My heart sank as I stepped through the doorway.

The apartment looked like a tornado had torn through it. Couch cushions slashed open, stuffing everywhere. Aunt Mary Jane's boxed figurines dumped on the floor, many of them smashed. Kitchen cabinets hanging open, contents scattered. Papers everywhere—tenant files, maintenance records, personal documents—creating a carpet of chaos.

But it was the bedroom that made my knees weak.

Spray paint. Bright red, dripping down my bedroom wall in angry letters two feet high: "FINAL WARNING."

I stood in the doorway, unable to move, unable to process what I was seeing. Someone had been in my home. Touched my things. Destroyed my space. Violated the one place I should have felt safe.

"Crystal." Lance's hand on my shoulder made me jump. "I need you to step back into the hallway. Don't touch anything. Martinez is on his way."

I let him guide me out, my movements mechanical. My brain felt fuzzy, disconnected from my body. This couldn't be real. This couldn't be happening.

"My notes," I said suddenly, the fog clearing. "I had notes about the investigation. Everything Linda told me, things I'd observed, timelines I'd worked out. They were on my desk."

Lance went back into the apartment, careful to step only where he'd already walked, and checked the desk. When he returned, his expression was grim.

"They're gone. Whoever did this took them."

"Why?" My voice cracked. "Why would someone take my notes? The police have all the same information. Martinez knows everything I know."

"Because they're scared." Lance kept his hand on my shoulder, anchoring me. "They're trying to intimidate you into stopping, and they wanted to know what you'd figured out. What you might have written down that could incriminate them."

Martinez arrived with a team of crime scene technicians five minutes later. He took one look at the apartment, and his jaw tightened.

"Ms. Waters, are you alright?"

I nodded, not trusting my voice.

"I need you to do a walk-through and tell me if anything is missing besides the notes. Don't touch anything. Just look."

The walk-through was surreal. Seeing my destroyed home, my scattered possessions, knowing that someone had rifled through my underwear drawer, pawed through my personal papers, stood in my bedroom with a can of spray paint and malice in their heart.

"Nothing valuable is gone," I reported when we finished. "My laptop is still here. The cash I kept in the kitchen drawer. Aunt Mary Jane's jewelry box—it's been opened, but nothing's missing."

"They weren't here to rob you," Martinez said. "This was targeted. Specific. They wanted those notes, and they wanted to scare you."

"Mission accomplished," I muttered.

Martinez pulled me aside while the techs started processing the scene. "Ms. Waters, I need you to stop investigating. No more following up on leads, no more interviewing suspects, no more playing detective. This is serious now. Someone broke into your home. They're escalating."

"I haven't been—"

"Yes, you have." His tone was firm but not unkind. "You and Lance have been conducting interviews, gathering information, piecing things together. And I've appreciated the help, truly. But it's putting you in danger. Whoever did this knows you're getting close to something. Let us handle it from here."

Lance appeared at my elbow. "She can't stay here tonight. The techs need at least four hours to process everything, and even after they're done, she can't sleep in a ransacked apartment with 'FINAL WARNING' on her wall."

"Agreed." Martinez looked at me. "Do you have somewhere you can stay? Family? Friends?"

"She's staying with me," Lance said before I could answer. "My apartment. It's close, secure, and I can keep an eye on her."

Martinez studied us both for a moment, then nodded. "That works. Ms. Waters, pack a bag—just clothes and toiletries. Don't take anything that might be evidence."

I moved through my destroyed apartment in a daze, gathering what I needed. Sensing my distress, the dogs huddled in a corner.

"Oh, babies." I dropped to my knees, and they swarmed me, whining and licking, their whole bodies trembling. "I'm so sorry."

Lance helped me gather the dogs and their supplies—food, bowls, toys, beds. By the time we made it to his apartment across the courtyard, I was operating on pure autopilot.

His apartment felt like a sanctuary after the violation of mine. Clean, organized, safe. He settled me on the couch while he set up food and water for the dogs.

"I'll make coffee," he said, heading for the kitchen.

I sat there, numb, watching my three dachshunds explore their new temporary home. They seemed to relax almost immediately, sensing the safety of the space. King lay down near them, a gentle guardian.

When Lance returned with coffee, I finally let myself feel it—the fear, the anger, the bone-deep violation of having my home invaded.

"They were in my bedroom," I whispered. "They went through my things."

Lance sat beside me, close enough that our shoulders touched. "But you're safe now. You're here, the dogs are here, and I'm not letting anyone get to you."

"What if they come here? What if they know I'm staying with you?"

"Then they'll have to get through me. And King. And the three attack dachshunds." The last part was said with a slight smile, trying to lighten the moment.

Despite everything, I almost smiled. "Fierce protectors."

"The fiercest." His hand found mine, fingers

intertwining. "Crystal, I need you to promise me something. No more investigating. No more following leads or interviewing suspects. Let Martinez handle it."

I haven't been—" I started, then stopped. Because that was a lie. "Okay. I promise. I'm done playing detective."

"Good." He squeezed my hand. "Now, you should try to rest. You've had a shock. I'll wake you if Martinez calls with updates. Take a hot shower and get out of those wet clothes. Should I ask?"

I scoffed. "Me being clumsy." I headed for the shower. Once I'd changed into dry clothes, I lay on Lance's bed with my three fur babies.

But I couldn't rest. Every time I closed my eyes, I saw that spray-painted message. FINAL WARNING. What happened after the final warning? When warnings stopped, and action began?

The afternoon dragged into the evening. Martinez called twice with updates. No fingerprints found. Whoever broke in had worn gloves. No security camera footage, they'd come in through the patio door, which faced the woods.

Lance ordered Chinese food for dinner, and we ate mostly in silence. I couldn't taste anything, just mechanically chewed and swallowed because I knew I should eat.

"I should call my parents," I said suddenly. "Let them know what's happening."

"Do they live nearby?"

"Florida. They retired there two years ago." I pulled out my phone, then hesitated. "If I tell them about this, they'll worry. They'll want me to come stay with them, to leave Riverside Towers."

"Would that be so bad?" Lance asked gently. "Temporarily, until this is resolved?"

I thought about it. Running away to Florida, letting someone else deal with the property, the investigation, the threats. It would be safe. Smart, even.

But it would also feel like letting the killer win.

"I'm not leaving," I said firmly. "This is my home. My property. My responsibility. I'm not letting them scare me away. And I won't put my parents at risk by asking them to come."

Something flickered in Lance's expression. Respect, maybe, or concern. "Then we do this together. You're not alone in this."

That night, I lay on Lance's couch, wrapped in a soft blanket he'd pulled from his closet. It smelled like him—clean laundry and that subtle cologne I'd come to associate with safety. Minnie was curled against my side, her warm body pressed against my ribs. Daisy and Bella had claimed the foot of the couch, tiny snoring lumps under the blanket.

King lay on the floor nearby, his eyes half-open, alert even in rest.

And Lance sat in the armchair across the room, fully dressed, a book open in his lap but his eyes on the door.

"You should sleep," I said quietly. "You don't have to stay up."

"I'm not tired." A lie, obvious from the shadows under his eyes. "Besides, someone should keep watch."

"Lance—"

"I can't." His voice was rough. "I can't close my eyes and risk something happening to you. Not after today. Not after seeing what they did to your home." He met my gaze across the dimly lit room. "So, I'm going to sit here and watch that door and make sure nothing and no one gets past me. That's not negotiable."

The fierceness in his voice made my chest tight. "Thank you," I whispered.

"Don't thank me. This is... I need to do this. I need to know you're safe."

I watched him for a while, this man who'd become so important to me in such a short time. Who'd searched the woods for my dog, who'd held me when I was scared, who now refused to sleep because he was too busy protecting me.

"Lance?" I said softly.

"Yeah?"

"When this is over... we should talk. About us."

In the dim light from the kitchen, I saw him smile. "Yeah. We should."

I closed my eyes and listened to the quiet sounds of the apartment. King's occasional shift of position, the puppies' soft snores, the rustle of pages as Lance pretended to read. Outside, a patrol car sat in the parking lot, another layer of protection Martinez had insisted on.

For the first time in days, despite everything that had happened, I felt safe.

Across the room, Lance set down his book and settled deeper into the chair, his eyes never leaving the door. His service weapon was within easy reach on the side table. King's ears twitched, tracking every sound from the hallway outside.

They would sit vigil all night—man and dog, guardian and protector.

And in the morning, we'd face whatever came next.

Together.

But for now, wrapped in Lance's blanket with Minnie's heartbeat steady against my side and the certain knowledge that someone was watching over me, I let myself rest.

The final warning had been given.

Now we just had to survive whatever came after it.

Around three AM, I woke to find Lance still in the chair, his head tilted back, eyes closed, but his posture still alert—the kind of sleep soldiers learned, where the body rested, but the mind stayed ready to react. His hand rested on his weapon.

I watched him for a moment, this man who'd literally given up sleep to keep me safe, and felt something shift in my chest. Something bigger than gratitude, deeper than friendship.

Something I wasn't quite ready to name but couldn't deny anymore.

"Sleep," I whispered, knowing he couldn't hear me. "I'm safe. You can rest."

But he didn't. Even in half-sleep, he kept watch.

And I fell back asleep knowing that whatever happened tomorrow, whatever danger still lurked out there, I had Lance Hendricks on my side.

It would have to be enough.

In the quiet dark of Lance's apartment with three dachshunds snoring peacefully and a German Shepherd standing guard, we were safe.

And that was everything.

Chapter Thirteen

I woke to the smell of coffee and bacon, disoriented for a moment about where I was. Then memory crashed back—the ransacked apartment, the spray-painted warning, sleeping on Lance's couch with three dachshunds as my bodyguards.

Already dressed in jeans and a navy henley, Lance flipped bacon in a pan. King sat nearby, his eyes tracking every movement of the food with laser focus.

"Morning." Lance glanced over his shoulder. "Hope you're hungry."

"Starving, actually." I sat up, careful not to disturb Minnie, who still curled against my side. My neck ached from the couch, but I'd slept better than I had in days. Something about knowing Lance watched over me had let me truly rest.

"Martinez called while you were sleeping. They're finished processing your apartment. You can go back whenever you're ready." Lance plated the bacon and started scrambling eggs. "Though I'd be happy to have you stay here as long as you need."

The casual way he said it, like having me in his space was no inconvenience at all, made my chest warm. "Thank you. For everything. For last night, for breakfast, for—"

A sharp knock on the door interrupted me. Lance's hand immediately went to his service weapon on the counter, and King stood at attention.

"Stay back." Lance moved toward the door.

He checked the peephole, then relaxed slightly. "It's Linda."

Linda? At seven thirty in the morning? That couldn't be good.

When Lance opened the door, Linda practically vibrated with barely contained information. She wore workout clothes and had five dogs on leashes, but clearly exercise wasn't her primary mission this morning.

"Crystal! Thank God you're here. I heard about your apartment, that's awful, but that's not why I'm here. Well, it is, sort of, but there's something else you need to know." She took a breath, finally noticing Lance standing there shirtless...no, wait, he was wearing a shirt, I was just imagining things because I was tired. "Can I come in? This is kind of important."

Lance stepped back, and Linda entered with her menagerie of dogs who immediately started investigating every corner of the apartment. My three dachshunds woke up and began barking, creating instant chaos.

"Linda," I said over the noise, "what's going on?"

"My boyfriend—you know, Derek, he works dispatch at the police station—he told me something last night that he probably shouldn't have, but he knows I walk dogs at the park, and he thought I should be aware for safety reasons." She paused for dramatic effect. "They found traffic camera footage of Victoria Thornton's car near the park at 9:45 PM the night Richard was killed."

My heart stopped. "What?"

"I know! Her car was photographed by the traffic camera on Elmwood and Maple, which is only two blocks from the park entrance. 9:45 PM, Crystal. That's right in the middle of the murder window." Linda's eyes gleamed with the thrill of sharing explosive gossip. "Her alibi was that she was at a charity gala in San Francisco, but the camera doesn't lie."

Lance had gone very still. "Did your boyfriend say if Martinez knows about this?"

"He's the one who found the footage. They're planning to bring Victoria in for questioning today, but Derek said they want to build a stronger case first. Search her home, her car, gather more evidence." Linda leaned in conspiratorially. "But here's the thing. Victoria doesn't know they have this footage yet. She thinks her alibi is solid."

I exchanged glances with Lance. If Victoria didn't

know the police had evidence placing her at the scene, we had a window of opportunity. But for what?

"Linda," Lance said carefully, "you need to keep this information to yourself. Don't spread it around. This is an active murder investigation."

"Oh, I know. I'm only telling you because, well, you're right in the middle of it." She gestured at me. "Someone broke into your apartment yesterday, Crystal. Whoever killed Richard is coming after you. You deserve to know that the prime suspect lied about her whereabouts."

After Linda left—reluctantly, clearly hoping for more drama—Lance and I stood in his kitchen staring at each other.

"We need to tell Martinez," Lance said.

"He already knows. Linda said he found the footage."

"But he doesn't know that Linda knows, which means he doesn't know that we know, and there could be operational security concerns..." Lance ran a hand through his hair, frustrated. "This is why civilians shouldn't be involved in active investigations."

"Says the civilian consultant," I pointed out.

"That's different. I'm trained. I know protocols." But his lips twitched, almost smiling.

I paced his small living room, my mind racing. Victoria had lied about her alibi. She'd been at the park during the murder. She'd written that threatening letter. She'd made a $50,000 cash withdrawal. Every piece of evidence pointed to her.

But something nagged at me. If Victoria had hired someone to kill Richard, why go to the park herself? Why risk being seen, being caught on camera? It didn't make sense.

"We should talk to her," I said suddenly.

Lance's expression shifted from thoughtful to alarmed. "Absolutely not."

"Hear me out." I crossed my arms. "Martinez is going to bring her in for questioning, but she'll lawyer up immediately. She'll deny everything, claim the traffic camera is wrong, or that she was just driving through the area. But if we talk to her now, before she knows the police have this evidence, she might tell us the truth."

"Or she might be a killer who just broke into your apartment and spray-painted a warning on your wall," Lance countered. "Crystal, this is exactly what Martinez told you not to do. No more investigating."

"I'm not investigating. I'm just... asking questions."

"That's literally what investigating is." Lance narrowed his eyes. "No. It's too dangerous."

"Then come with me. You'll be there to make sure nothing happens." I met his eyes, willing him to understand. "Lance, someone is threatening me. I deserve to know if Victoria is behind it. And if we can get her to admit to being at the park that night, that's information Martinez can use."

"He doesn't need our help getting information. He's a professional detective with years of experience and the full resources of the police department."

"But he doesn't have the advantage we have right now. Victoria doesn't know we know about the camera footage. She thinks her alibi is solid. If we approach her as concerned residents, just asking about the investigation, she might let something slip."

Lance stared at me for a long moment, and I could see the internal battle playing out on his face. The cop in him said to follow protocol, report to Martinez, and let the professionals handle it. But something else— maybe his feelings for me, maybe his own desire to protect me by confirming Victoria was the threat— made him hesitate.

"If we do this," he finally said, "we do it together. You don't go anywhere near her without me. And the second it feels dangerous, we leave and call Martinez. Agreed?"

"Agreed." I grinned.

Victoria lived in one of the luxury penthouses downtown, the kind with a doorman, a marble lobby, and an elevator that required a key card to access the upper floors. We had to call from the lobby phone to get buzzed up.

"Yes?" Victoria's voice came through, smooth and polished even over the intercom.

"Mrs. Thornton, it's Crystal Waters and Lance Hendricks from Riverside Towers. We need to speak with you about the investigation. It's urgent."

A pause. Then, "Come up."

The elevator ride to the fifteenth floor felt interminable. Lance stood close to me, his body language protective, his hand resting near where his service weapon sat in a concealed holster.

"Let me do most of the talking," he said quietly. "And stay near the door. If anything feels wrong, we leave immediately."

Victoria opened her penthouse door wearing white linen pants and a silk blouse, her hair perfectly styled, makeup flawless. She looked like someone preparing for a photo shoot, not someone about to be questioned about murder.

"Come in." She stepped back. "Though I must say, this is unexpected. I thought the police had finished with their questions."

The penthouse was stunning. Floor-to-ceiling windows with views of the city, modern furniture in whites and grays, art that probably cost more than my entire apartment complex. Everything was sterile and perfect and cold.

Victoria gestured to a white leather couch. "Please, sit. Can I offer you anything? Coffee? Water?"

"No, thank you." I perched on the edge of the couch, very aware of how expensive it probably was. Lance remained standing, positioning himself between Victoria and me.

"Mrs. Thornton," I began, "we've learned some

information that concerns us. About the night Richard was killed."

Her expression didn't change, but something flickered in her eyes. "Oh?"

"Traffic camera footage places your car near the park at 9:45 PM that night. You told police you were at a charity gala in San Francisco."

Lance cleared his throat in an attempt to get me to stop talking. He had told me he would do the talking, but I couldn't help myself.

The color drained from Victoria's face. For several seconds, she didn't speak, just stared at us with an expression that shifted from shock to fear to something like resignation.

"How did you…the police don't have that footage yet. They couldn't have." Her voice was barely above a whisper.

"They do," Lance said flatly. "And they're planning to bring you in for questioning. Today."

Victoria sank into a chair, all her polish crumbling. "I didn't kill him. You have to believe me. I didn't kill Richard."

"Then why did you lie about your alibi?" I tried to keep my voice gentle despite the anger simmering beneath. "Why were you at the park?"

"Because I'm an idiot." She laughed, a broken sound without humor. "Because I went to meet him. He called me that afternoon, said we needed to talk about the settlement. That he had new information that could change everything. He wanted to meet at the park, and said it would be private, neutral ground."

"So, you drove there from San Francisco," Lance said.

"No. I was never in San Francisco. I lied to everyone. Told my friends I was sick and couldn't attend the gala. I stayed home waiting for Richard's call." Victoria's hands twisted in her lap. "When he said to meet him at nine thirty, I went. I got there around 9:45, parked near the entrance, and walked to the spot he'd specified—near the lake, by that big oak tree."

My heart pounded. The spot where we'd found Thornton's body.

"And?" Lance prompted.

"And he was already dead." Victoria's voice broke. "He was lying there with blood everywhere, and I panicked. I knew how it would look. We were divorced, I'd made threats, and we were fighting over money. If anyone found out I was there, I'd be the prime suspect."

"So, you fled," I said.

"I ran. I got in my car and drove home and tried to pretend it never happened." Tears streamed down her face, ruining her perfect makeup. "I didn't kill him. I swear on everything I have, I didn't kill Richard. But I was there, and I found him, and I didn't report it, and now I look guilty of murder."

Lance and I exchanged glances. Her story was plausible. It explained the traffic camera footage, her lies about the gala, and her strange behavior since the murder. But it also conveniently placed her at the scene with no witnesses to corroborate her innocence.

"What about the threatening letter?" I asked. "The one that was buried with the wallet? The handwriting analysis matched yours."

Victoria's eyes widened. "What letter? What wallet? I don't know what you're talking about."

"The letter said, 'You know what you did. This is your last warning.' It was found buried near the crime scene with five thousand dollars cash." Lance's voice was hard. "The handwriting matched yours despite the disguise."

"That's impossible. I never wrote any letter. I never buried any money." Victoria stood abruptly. "Someone is framing me. Don't you see? Someone killed Richard, and they're setting me up to take the fall."

"Or you're lying," Lance said bluntly.

"I'm not!" Victoria's voice rose. "Yes, I was there. Yes, I found his body. Yes, I ran like a coward instead of calling the police. But I didn't kill him, and I certainly didn't write any threatening letters or bury cash like some bad movie plot."

"You need to tell Martinez all of this," I said. "Everything you just told us. Right now."

"They won't believe me. The evidence is too damning. Traffic camera, handwriting analysis, motive—" Victoria wrapped her arms around herself.

"I'll be arrested."

"You'll be arrested anyway when Martinez comes for you today," Lance said. "But if you come forward voluntarily, if you tell the truth, that might count for something."

"And if it doesn't? If they charge me with murder based on circumstantial evidence?" Victoria shot a desperate look between us. "Please. I'm begging you. Don't tell the police about this conversation. Give me twenty-four hours to find a lawyer, to prepare. Just one day."

"No." Lance shook his head.

"Please. I didn't kill anyone. I'm not a threat to you or anyone else. Twenty-four hours won't make any difference to the investigation, but it could make all the difference to me."

I could feel Lance's eyes on me, waiting for me to back him up, to agree that we should call Martinez immediately. And part of me, the rational, cautious part, knew he was right.

But another part of me looked at Victoria's tear-stained face and saw genuine terror. What if she told the truth? What if she had stumbled onto a crime scene and panicked, and now someone was framing her for murder?

"We should give her a chance to come forward herself," I said quietly.

Lance's head snapped toward me. "What?"

"If she turns herself in voluntarily, that looks

better than being arrested. It shows cooperation, remorse for not reporting what she found. Give her until tomorrow morning to get a lawyer and go to the police on her own terms."

"Crystal." Lance's voice was tight. "Can I speak with you in the hallway?"

In the penthouse corridor, with Victoria's door closed, Lance turned to face me. "What are you doing?"

"Giving her a chance—"

"She's a murder suspect! She lied about her alibi; she was at the scene, all the evidence points to her, and you want to give her twenty-four hours to run?"

"She won't run. Where would she go? Martinez already has surveillance on her, I'm sure of it." I crossed my arms. "Lance, what if she's telling the truth? What if she really did just find the body and panic?"

"Then she should have reported it immediately. By running, by lying, she made herself look guilty. And by confronting her, we've now potentially tipped off a killer that the police are onto her."

"Or we've given an innocent woman a chance to get proper legal representation before being railroaded by circumstantial evidence." My voice rose. "Not everyone who makes bad decisions is a murderer."

"No, but some of them are." Lance's jaw was set, his eyes hard. "This is protocol, Crystal. When you have a suspect who's lied about their alibi and placed themselves at a crime scene, you bring them in immediately. You don't give them time to destroy evidence or flee or get their story straight with a lawyer."

"I'm not a cop. I don't have to follow protocol."

"But I do. Or I'm supposed to." He ran a hand through his hair in frustration. "Martinez is going to kill me for this. For letting you talk me into confronting a suspect, for not calling it in immediately, for—"

"I didn't talk you into anything. You agreed to come here."

"Because I wanted to keep you safe! Because I knew you'd probably do something reckless like this whether I was here or not!" His voice echoed in the quiet hallway.

We stared at each other, the space between us suddenly feeling like a canyon. This was our first real disagreement. Not a small thing, but something fundamental—different approaches to justice, to risk, to the right way to handle a dangerous situation.

"I'm calling Martinez," Lance said finally. "Now. And I'm telling him everything. That Victoria was at the scene, that she admitted to finding the body, that we confronted her without backup like idiots."

"Fine." I turned toward the elevator. "But I'm giving her a heads up first. She deserves that much."

"Crystal—"

I didn't wait to hear the rest. I knocked on Victoria's door, and when she opened it, her face hopeful, I said quickly: "Lance is calling Detective Martinez now. If you're going to get a lawyer and turn yourself in voluntarily, you need to do it today. Don't wait. Don't run. Just get representation and tell them the truth."

"Thank you," she whispered.

By the time I reached the elevator, Lance was already on the phone with Martinez. I could hear his clipped, professional tone as he reported every detail of our unauthorized interview.

The elevator ride down was silent. Lance stood on one side, phone still to his ear, not looking at me. I stood on the other, arms crossed, trying not to feel hurt by his anger.

Chemistry was easy when you agreed on everything. But what happened when you didn't? When instinct pulled you in different directions?

Martinez was waiting for us in the lobby, his expression thunderous.

"My office," he said. "Both of you. Now."

The ride to the police station was agonizing. Lance drove, his hands tight on the wheel. I sat in the passenger seat, watching the city pass by, wondering if we'd just made everything worse.

And wondering if the distance I felt between us now was temporary, a disagreement to be worked through, or something more fundamental that couldn't be bridged.

Either way, Victoria Thornton's world was about to come crashing down around her, and Lance and I had just had our first fight.

It remained to be seen which situation would be easier to resolve.

Chapter Fourteen

As if he hadn't got enough of us, Martinez called us back into his office the next morning. His lecture lasted forty-five minutes. Forty-five minutes of him explaining, in excruciating detail, why confronting murder suspects without backup was dangerous, why giving said suspects advance warning was obstruction of justice, and why civilians, even well-meaning ones, should leave police work to the police.

Lance took it stoically, his expression carefully neutral. I squirmed in my chair, feeling like a teenager being scolded by a disappointed parent.

"However," Martinez finally said, and both our heads snapped up, "Victoria Thornton did turn herself in this morning with her lawyer. She gave a statement matching what she told you. That she found Richard's body and panicked. We're holding her as a person of interest, but without physical evidence placing her at the actual murder, we can't charge her yet."

"So, she might be telling the truth?" I asked.

"She might be lying very convincingly." Martinez leaned back in his chair. "The handwriting analysis is still bothering me. Those patterns don't lie. But she's adamant she never wrote that letter, and her lawyer is already preparing to challenge the analysis."

"What about the $50,000 withdrawal?" Lance asked.

"Claimed it was for a remodel of her vacation home. She's providing receipts, contractor information. It might check out, or it might be a cover story." Martinez pulled out a file. "But there's another development. One you two should know about since you seem determined to involve yourselves in this investigation regardless of my warnings."

He slid a photograph across the desk. A man in his fifties with graying temples, an expensive suit, and a smile that didn't reach his eyes.

"David Reeves. Richard Thornton's business partner in Thornton-Reeves Development Corporation." Martinez tapped the photo. "We've been looking into everyone in Richard's orbit, and Reeves keeps pinging our radar."

"Linda mentioned him at the dog park," I said, remembering. "She pointed him out as someone who worked for Thornton."

"Not just worked for. Partnered with. Equal ownership, equal say in business decisions. Except Richard was the face of the company while David handled the financial side." Martinez pulled out more documents. "Two weeks before the murder, Richard contacted a forensic accountant. He suspected David of embezzling company funds."

Lance sat forward. "How much are we talking?"

"Over $2 million over the past three years. Small amounts at first, then increasingly larger as he got bolder. Richard had just received preliminary findings confirming the embezzlement. He was planning to go to the police and the board of directors the week after he died."

My stomach dropped. "David had a motive. Prison time and losing everything if Richard exposed him."

"Exactly. And here's where it gets interesting. David has no alibi for the night of the murder. Claims he was home alone, working. No one to verify it." Martinez pulled out another document. "And a bartender at The Copper Room downtown remembers David and Richard arguing there the evening before the murder. Got heated enough that the bartender almost kicked them out."

"What were they arguing about?" I asked.

"According to the bartender, Richard said something about 'doing the right thing,' and David responded, 'I'll stop you before you destroy me.'" Martinez looked between us. "That's not an idle threat. That's a man desperate enough to kill."

Lance studied the documents, his cop brain

clearly working through the implications. "What's David's background? Any history of violence?"

"Clean record. But that doesn't mean much. First-time killers exist, especially when they're backed into a corner." Martinez closed the file. "We're bringing him in for questioning this afternoon. I wanted you to know because—" he looked at me specifically, "—you live at Riverside Towers. David Reeves has been there multiple times. He knew Richard was interested in the property. He might see you as a problem, just like Victoria did."

The reminder that I was potentially on a killer's radar made my skin crawl. "You think he's the one who broke into my apartment?"

"I think whoever killed Richard is desperate. Desperate people do desperate things." Martinez stood. "Go home. Stay alert. And for the love of God, stop confronting murder suspects without calling me first."

In Lance's truck on the way back to Riverside Towers, the silence was heavy. We hadn't really talked since our disagreement at Victoria's penthouse, and the tension sat between us like a physical thing.

"I'm sorry," I finally said. "About yesterday. About arguing with you in front of Victoria, about giving her that warning. You were right. It was reckless."

Lance's hands tightened on the steering wheel. "I'm sorry too. I shouldn't have yelled at you in the hallway. You were trying to be compassionate, to give someone a chance. That's not wrong, it's just... different from how I'd handle it."

"Different approaches," I said quietly.

"Yeah." He pulled into the Riverside parking lot but didn't turn off the engine. "Crystal, there's something you should know. About why I'm so rigid about protocol, about following the rules even when it seems heartless."

I waited, sensing this was important.

"My partner, Jake Martinez, actually, the detective's younger brother, was killed eight months ago during a botched arrest." Lance's voice was flat, emotionless, his knuckles white on the steering wheel. "We had a warrant to bring in a suspect for questioning. Standard pickup that should have been routine. But I didn't follow protocol."

"Lance—"

"I had a gut feeling something was off. The suspect was too calm, too cooperative. I wanted to call for backup, but the warrant said two officers were sufficient. Jake thought I was overthinking it, being paranoid. We went in without additional support." He closed his eyes. "The suspect had a gun hidden. Jake went through the door first. He was shot twice before either of us could react."

My heart broke for him. "That wasn't your fault."

"I knew something was wrong. My instincts were screaming at me. If I'd called for backup anyway, if I'd insisted we wait, if I'd gone through that door first—"

His voice cracked. "Jake died because I ignored my gut and followed the rules. And I got a knee full of rebar when I fell through that rotted floor trying to pursue the shooter."

"Is that why Martinez has been so tolerant of our involvement?" I asked softly. "Because you're his brother's partner?"

"Former partner. I'm on medical leave, remember? But yeah, Martinez knows I blame myself. He doesn't blame me. He's said that a hundred times. The suspect killed Jake, not me. But knowing it intellectually doesn't make the guilt go away."

I unbuckled my seatbelt and shifted to face him. "Lance, you can't blame yourself for following protocol. That's an impossible standard."

"But don't you see? That's why this morning at Victoria's was so hard for me. You wanted to follow your instincts, show compassion, and give her a chance. And part of me agreed with you. But the other part, the part that watched Jake die, screamed that we needed to follow protocol, call it in, do everything by the book because that's how you stay safe and keep others safe." He finally looked at me, pain raw in his dark eyes. "I'm terrified that if I trust my instincts again, if I break protocol for the right reasons, someone else will die."

"So, you overcorrect." Understanding dawned. "You follow the rules rigidly because you're afraid of what happens when you don't."

"Yeah." He laughed, a broken sound. "I'm a mess,

basically. A broken cop who can't trust himself enough to do his job anymore."

"You're not broken." I reached over and took his hand. "You're grieving. You're dealing with trauma. And you're still helping, still protecting people, still making a difference. Jake's death wasn't your fault, and neither was your injury. You were doing your job."

"Tell that to the nightmares." But his fingers curled around mine, holding tight. "I see him every night, Crystal. Going through that door. The gun firing. Him falling. And I can't—I can't go back to active duty if I can't trust my judgment. If I freeze up at the critical moment, more people will die."

We sat in the truck, hands clasped, while Lance's pain filled the space between us. I finally understood why he'd been so closed off when we first met. Why he'd seemed so lost despite his competence. Why he needed the structure and rules and protocol so badly.

Jake Martinez's death had broken something in Lance Hendricks. And he wasn't sure if it could be fixed.

"Thank you," he finally said. "For listening. For not telling me I'm being ridiculous or that I should just get over it."

"You're not ridiculous. You're human." I squeezed his hand. "And for what it's worth, I think Jake would be proud of how you're still fighting. Still trying to do good despite being hurt and scared and grieving."

"Maybe." He took a shaky breath, then seemed to

pull himself together. "We should look into David Reeves. Martinez said he's bringing him in this afternoon, but there might be information we can find before then. Public records, social media, anything that might help build a picture of who he is."

"Are you sure? We just got lectured about interfering—"

"Research isn't interfering. It's being prepared." Lance managed a small smile. "Besides, I need something to focus on besides my own head. Come on."

We spent the next three hours in Lance's apartment, laptops open, digging through everything we could find on David Reeves. My three dachshunds napped on the couch, King sprawled on the floor, while we worked at the kitchen table.

David Reeves had a carefully curated online presence. Professional headshots, articles about successful development projects, photos at charity galas, and golf tournaments. Nothing controversial. Nothing suspicious.

"Too clean." Lance scrolled through David's social media. "Nobody's this boring."

I pulled up court records. "He's been sued three times in the past five years. All civil cases related to construction contracts. Two settled out of court, one dismissed."

"Pattern of cutting corners?" Lance made notes. "Or just the nature of the development business?"

"Could be either." I clicked on another link. "Oh, this is interesting. David declared bankruptcy twelve years ago. Lost everything in a bad real estate deal."

Lance looked up sharply. "So, he knows what it's like to lose everything. And he's about to lose it all again if Richard exposes the embezzlement."

We kept digging, building a profile. David Reeves: fifty-three years old, divorced twice, no children. He'd built his way back from bankruptcy through careful investments and his partnership with Richard Thornton. The development company was worth millions, and David owned half of it.

"Everything he's built over the past decade would be gone," I said. "Prison time for embezzlement, loss of the company, bankruptcy again. He'd have nothing."

"Strong motive for murder." Lance pulled up the bartender's statement about the argument. "'I'll stop you before you destroy me.' That's pretty clear intent."

"But how does Victoria fit in? The traffic camera, the handwriting on the letter?"

"Maybe she's telling the truth. Maybe she really did find the body and panic." Lance rubbed his eyes, fatigue catching up with him. "Or maybe David and Victoria worked together. She writes the threatening letter, he does the actual killing, they both have deniability."

My phone rang—Martinez.

"We just finished interviewing David Reeves," the detective said without preamble. "He's admitted to the embezzlement. He claimed he was planning to pay it all back, that he'd gotten in over his head with gambling debts. But he swears he didn't kill Richard."

"Do you believe him?"

"I believe he embezzled over $2 million. Everything else is still being verified." Martinez paused. "Ms. Waters, David mentioned you specifically. Said Richard had talked about trying to buy Riverside Towers from your aunt. When I asked if he'd ever approached you about selling, he got defensive. Said the property was worth more to him than it would ever be to you."

My blood ran cold. "He threatened me?"

"Not directly. But the implication was there. I want you to stay away from him. If he shows up at Riverside, you call me immediately."

After hanging up, I relayed the conversation to Lance, who looked grim.

"David sees you as an obstacle," he said. "Just like Martinez warned. If he killed Richard to protect himself, he might come after you to protect the property deal."

"But I'm not even planning to sell. The property isn't going anywhere."

"He doesn't know that. Or he thinks he can pressure you, threaten you, force you to sell." Lance's jaw was set. "You're not going back to your apartment alone. Not until David is cleared or arrested."

"Lance, I can't keep staying here. You need your

space—”

“I need you safe.” He took my hand again, his grip firm. “After everything I just told you, after Jake, after knowing what it feels like to lose someone…I can't lose you too, Crystal. I won't.”

The intensity in his voice made my breath catch. This wasn't just about protection, duty, or even friendship. This was something deeper, something we'd been dancing around since we met.

“Okay,” I whispered. “I'll stay.”

“Good.” He didn't release my hand. “We figure out who killed Richard. We make sure you're safe. And then...”

“Then we talk about us,” I finished.

“Yeah. Then we talk about us.”

Outside, rain started falling, tapping against the windows. Inside, surrounded by research about murder suspects and embezzlement, sitting at Lance's kitchen table with our hands joined, something fundamental shifted between us.

We'd had our first fight. We'd seen each other's pain, fears, and flaws.

And somehow, that made what we had more real.

Not perfect. Not without complications, differences, or challenges.

But real.

And worth fighting for—both the investigation and whatever was growing between us.

My phone buzzed with a text from Martinez:

"David Reeves released. Insufficient evidence to hold. Be careful."

I showed Lance, and his expression darkened.

"Then we dig deeper," he said. "We find the evidence Martinez needs. Together."

"Together," I agreed.

Because despite our different approaches, despite the danger, despite everything that could go wrong—we were better together than apart.

And whoever killed Richard Thornton was about to find that out.

Chapter Fifteen

"**Drop that sock.**" I chased Bella around the apartment until she let go of my sock in her dog bed and wagged her tail as if she'd done something proud. "No stealing." I wagged my finger at her, which she promptly licked. Despite my annoyance, I smiled. How could I resist that face?

Shaking my head at her shenanigans, I put leashes on the three dogs. "Not that the three of you deserve time at the dog park, but the exercise won't hurt any of us. Behave, or I'll bring you straight back here."

It had been two days since Martinez released David Reeves, two days of looking over my shoulder and jumping at shadows. Lance had barely left my side, working from his laptop at my kitchen table. Well, his kitchen table, since I was still staying at his apartment at night, I would only go to my apartment to handle tenant issues during the day.

But this morning, the walls were closing in. I

needed fresh air, sunshine, and normalcy. And my three dachshunds were going stir-crazy from being cooped up.

"We'll be quick," I'd promised Lance when he'd given me that look—the one that said he wanted to argue but knew I needed this. "Thirty minutes, just a quick walk to the dog park and back."

"Keep your phone on. Call me if anything seems off." He'd kissed my forehead, a gesture that was becoming increasingly natural between us. "I mean it, Crystal. Anything. I've got some things to do, but I won't be gone long."

Now, standing in his apartment doorway with three excited dogs, I felt almost normal. Almost like a regular person taking her pets for a walk, not someone being hunted by a killer.

A frenzy of barks ensued as I opened the door and stepped outside into the crisp morning air. The sun was just fully up, casting long shadows across the courtyard. Most residents were still asleep or getting ready for work, giving the complex a peaceful quiet.

A rabbit darted across our path near the flower beds I'd planted weeks ago. All three dogs took off at once, yanking their leashes from my hands with surprising force, and raced after the poor rabbit, me hot on their heels.

"Stop, you naughty dogs!" Of course, they ignored me. Their prey drive had kicked in, turning my usually manageable dachshunds into tiny hunting machines. Daisy reached the poor animal first, her jaws snapping inches from its fluffy tail. I grabbed her and pulled her back as the rabbit squeezed through the gate around the pool, disappearing into the safety of the landscaping beyond. "Come on. Let's get to the park so the poor rabbit can go home."

I held the leashes tighter this time, wrapping them around my wrist for extra security, and let the dogs lead the way. They pulled hard, still excited from the chase, their little legs pumping as we headed down the sidewalk toward the dog park three blocks away.

If this was any indication of how my day was going to go, I ought to go back to bed.

The morning was beautiful, though. Cool but not cold, with that quality of light that made everything look fresh and new. A few joggers passed us, and a woman walking a golden retriever waved. Normal. Safe.

The dog park came into view, the familiar chain-link fence and scattered benches welcoming. Usually, by 7:30 AM, there would be a handful of early risers with their dogs. Linda often came around this time, I knew, with whatever collection of clients' dogs she would watch that day.

But as we approached, something felt off.

There were several dogs running around the dog park, barking and playing with each other, but I didn't see any humans. Not at first. The dogs seemed unsupervised, which was strange and against park rules.

Then I spotted someone lying on the bench of a far picnic table against the fence. My first thought was of a homeless person. We occasionally had people sleeping in the park overnight, but something about the figure's stillness made my stomach clench.

I unclicked the dogs from their leashes, letting them into the small dog enclosure, where they immediately started sniffing everything with enthusiasm. Then I headed toward the person I assumed was napping.

"I don't think you should sleep here," I called out as I got closer. "The park rangers—"

I stopped mid-sentence. The person wore yoga pants and a purple jacket. Linda's purple jacket. The one she'd worn the first day I met her.

"Linda?" My voice came out thin and scared.

I shook her shoulder gently, then more urgently as she didn't respond. She rolled over, and I gasped as I got a glimpse of Linda Harper's beaten and bloody face.

Her lip was split, blood dried in a dark line down her chin. One eye was swollen completely shut, already turning purple. Her nose looked broken, bent at an unnatural angle. More blood matted her hair on the left side.

"Linda!" I glanced around for help, but the park was empty except for the dogs. My hands shook as I pulled out my phone and called 911. "I need an ambulance at Riverside Dog Park. A woman's been attacked. She's breathing but unconscious. Hurry."

The operator's voice was calm and professional, asking questions I barely registered. How long had she been here? I didn't know. Was she responsive? Not really. Keep her warm, don't move her unless necessary. Help is on the way.

"Can you hear me?" I patted Linda's shoulder, trying to remember first aid training I'd taken years ago. ABC—airway, breathing, circulation. She was breathing. Her chest rose and fell. But she was hurt, badly hurt.

"Hmm hmm." A sound, barely audible.

"Linda, it's Crystal. You're going to be okay. Help is coming." I shrugged off my jacket and laid it over her, trying to keep her warm. "What happened?"

Her good eye fluttered open, trying to focus on me. "Someone... jumped me." The words came out slurred, possibly from pain or a concussion. "As soon as I... entered the park. This morning. I came early. Right after sunup because I have... things to do later today." She swiped the back of her hand across her nose, smearing blood. "I knew you'd said... You planned on coming this morning. Wanted to tell you something."

My blood ran cold. "Tell me what?"

"I dreamed... last night. I saw someone... at the park the night Thornton died." She lifted red-rimmed eyes to me, struggling to focus. "Then I realized it might not have been... a dream. But a memory. Someone was here. Someone I know."

I swallowed against the lump in my throat. Had I been the target or Linda? If Linda had information about the killer, if she'd seen something that night and were starting to remember, she'd become a threat. And if she'd been coming to tell me, then the killer might think I knew too.

Chills ran down my spine as I glanced again around the park. The trees suddenly looked menacing, the shadows deep enough to hide someone. Were they watching us right now? Waiting to see if Linda would say more?

"Who did you see?" I asked urgently. "Linda, who was it?"

But her eye had closed again, her breathing becoming shallow.

As sirens wailed in the distance, I dug a water bottle from my backpack and held it to Linda's lips. "Here. Help is on the way. Just hold on."

"Can't." Her eyes closed completely, and she fell to the ground, sliding off the bench.

I caught her, easing her down to the grass, my heart hammering. "Linda! Stay with me. Don't you dare die. Do you hear me? Don't you dare."

She didn't respond.

I felt for a pulse. There, faint but steady. Still breathing. But unconscious.

The ambulance arrived four minutes later, though it felt like hours. Two EMTs jumped out and immediately took over, asking rapid-fire questions I tried to answer while staying out of their way.

Lance arrived at the same time. He must have heard the sirens or tracked my phone. He took one look at Linda, at me, covered in her blood from catching her, and went pale.

"Crystal." He pulled me away from the EMTs, his hands on my shoulders, checking me over. "Are you hurt? Is this your blood?"

"No. It's Linda's. Someone attacked her. Beat her." My voice shook. "She was trying to tell me something about the night of the murder. She saw someone, Lance. She said she remembered."

His expression went from concerned to furious in an instant. "This was meant for you. Whoever did this thought Linda was you, or they attacked her to keep her quiet before she could tell you what she knew."

"We don't know—"

"We do know." His grip tightened. "Dark hair, similar build, at the park early morning. If someone was watching, waiting for you to show up alone like you said you might, they could have mistaken her for you. Or they knew she was coming to tell you something and had to stop her."

Martinez's car screeched into the parking lot, followed by two patrol cars. The detective emerged, his expression thunderous.

"Ms. Waters. Mr. Hendricks." He looked between us. "Tell me exactly what happened."

I recounted everything—finding Linda, her words

about the dream/memory, someone jumping her right when she entered the park. Martinez took notes, his jaw getting tighter with each detail.

"She said she saw someone that night," Martinez repeated. "Did she say who?"

"She passed out before she could tell me." Frustration and fear made my voice sharp. "She said it was someone she knows. Someone familiar."

"Which could be anyone in Riverside Towers or any regular at this park." Martinez watched as the EMTs loaded Linda onto a stretcher. "She's being taken to County General. I'll have officers stationed outside her room. If she wakes up, we'll get a statement."

"If she wakes up?" My voice cracked.

"When," Martinez corrected gently. "When she wakes up. The EMTs think she'll make it. Head injuries bleed a lot, look worse than they are sometimes. But she's in bad shape."

The EMTs wheeled Linda past us, her face now partially obscured by an oxygen mask. One of them checked her pupils with a light, the other adjusted IV bags.

"She has to make it," I whispered. "She has to."

After the ambulance left, Martinez walked the crime scene with his team. They found signs of a struggle near the park entrance: trampled grass and a dropped leash.

"Whoever did this is getting desperate," Martinez said. "Sloppy. This is an outdoor attack in a public place in broad daylight. That's high-risk behavior."

"Which means they're scared," Lance said. "Running out of time or options."

"Or both." Martinez turned to me. "Ms. Waters, I need to be very clear with you. You are in extreme danger. Whoever killed Richard Thornton has now attacked Linda Harper. They could be eliminating potential witnesses and anyone they perceive as a threat. You need to go somewhere safe. Out of town would be best."

"I'm not leaving—" I started.

"Then you're staying with police protection 24/7." Martinez's tone left no room for argument. "Lance, can she stay with you?"

"She has been. I'm not letting her out of my sight."

"Good. I'm assigning a patrol car to sit outside your building. You see anything suspicious, you call immediately." Martinez looked at me. "I need you to back off this investigation. Completely. No more research, no more talking to potential suspects, no more walks in the park alone. Understood?"

I nodded, too shaken to argue.

After Martinez left to coordinate with his team, Lance pulled me against his chest, his arms wrapping around me tight enough that I could barely breathe. But I didn't care. I needed the solid warmth of him, needed to feel safe even though I knew nowhere was truly safe right now.

"I'm not letting anything happen to you." His lips brushed against my hair. "Do you hear me? Nothing. I don't care what I have to do, who I have to fight, or what rules I have to break. You're not becoming the next victim."

"Lance—"

"I couldn't save Jake. I didn't protect him as I should have. But I will protect you. I swear it." His voice was rough with emotion and determination. "We're going to catch whoever did this. And until we do, you don't go anywhere without me. Not even to get the mail."

I pulled back enough to see his face. The fear and ferocity there took my breath away. This wasn't just professional protection or even friendship. This was something much deeper.

"Okay," I whispered. "I promise. No more solo adventures. No more risks."

"Good." He didn't release me, and I didn't want him to.

We stood there in the dog park while police processed the crime scene around us, holding each other like lifelines. My three dachshunds had finally calmed down and were pressing against our legs, sensing the tension.

Someone had tried to kill Linda. Whether they'd mistaken her for me or targeted her specifically, the message was clear. Anyone who knew anything about Richard Thornton's murder was in danger.

Which meant I was running out of time.

Either we caught the killer, or the killer would come for me next.

Later that afternoon at the hospital, we sat in uncomfortable plastic chairs in the waiting room. Linda was in surgery. They'd found internal bleeding and were working to stabilize her. Her ex-husband had been contacted and was on his way from two states over.

"She has to make it," I said for the hundredth time. "She has to tell us what she remembered."

"She will." Lance's hand found mine, our fingers intertwining automatically now. "She's a fighter. You should have seen her handling those five dogs at once. That takes strength."

A doctor emerged from the surgical wing, and we stood immediately. But she walked past us to another family, and we sank back down.

"This is my fault," I said quietly. "If I hadn't gotten involved, if I'd just let Martinez handle everything—"

"Then Linda still would have remembered seeing someone that night. She still would have been a target." Lance squeezed my hand. "This isn't your fault. It's the killer's fault. They chose to hurt people to protect themselves."

"But Linda came to tell me. She was trying to help me, to warn me, and now—"

"Now she's fighting for her life, and we're going to make sure her attacker pays for it." Lance's voice was steel. "When she wakes up and tells us who she saw, we're ending this. Together."

Hours passed. Lance got us coffee from the vending machine. Martinez called with updates. Still no leads on Linda's attacker, no witnesses had come forward, and the investigation was ongoing.

Finally, as the sun was setting, a surgeon emerged and approached us.

"She's stable. She made it through surgery. We had to relieve pressure on her brain from the head trauma, and she has several broken ribs and a fractured orbital bone. But she's alive, and the prognosis is cautiously optimistic."

Relief flooded through me so strongly that my knees went weak. Lance steadied me, his arm around my waist.

"Can we see her?" I asked.

"Not tonight. She's in the ICU and heavily sedated. Maybe tomorrow if she continues to improve." The surgeon gave us a tired smile. "She's lucky you found her when you did, Ms. Waters. Another hour and we might be having a very different conversation."

As we left the hospital, exhausted and emotionally drained, Lance kept his arm around me. The patrol car Martinez promised was waiting in his parking lot when we arrived. The officer inside gave us a nod.

Inside Lance's apartment, I collapsed on the couch. The three dogs immediately swarmed me, providing warm, furry comfort.

Lance sat beside me, pulling me against his side. "We're close," he said. "Whoever did this is panicking. They're making mistakes. We're going to catch them."

"Before they catch us?"

"Before they catch you." He tilted my chin up, forcing me to meet his eyes. "I promise you, Crystal. You're going to survive this. We both are."

He pressed a kiss to my forehead, gentle and sweet and full of promise. "Now rest. Tomorrow, we figure out who Linda saw."

I closed my eyes, surrounded by warmth and protection and the quiet certainty that whatever came next, we'd face it together.

The danger had reached critical levels. But so had our determination to find Thornton's killer and who had hurt Linda.

Chapter Sixteen

I stared at a black-and-white kitten stuck in a tree. How in heaven's name was I supposed to get the poor thing down? Since my three yapping dogs weren't helping, I shut them in my apartment and returned to the tree.

I suppose I could call the fire department, but coaxing a cat with treats ought to work. I pulled a dog treat from my pocket. "Here, kittie, kittie."

A meow was the only response.

"What's going on?" Lance stepped up next to me.

"That. I'm trying to coax it down. It's scared out of its mind."

"Hmmm." Lance glanced around.

The kitten slipped, and I gasped, before it managed to secure its perch again. "We need to do something quick."

"Get on my shoulders."

"What?" I widened my eyes.

"You don't look like you weigh much. I'll boost you up, and you get the cat." Lance grinned.

Heaven help me, but another frightened meow from the kitten spurred me to climb onto Lance's shoulders like a monkey. I held out the treat, hoping to lure the poor thing closer since she was still just out of reach.

Betty Henderson, still in her robe with curlers in her hair, joined us. "What tomfoolery are the two of you up to?"

"Cat," I answered without looking down.

The kitten hissed, yowled, and then launched itself from the tree branch onto the top of Betty's head. The woman shrieked and spun, trying to remove the kitten, whose nails were firmly planted in the hair curlers.

I slid from Lance's shoulders and rushed to help, since he was doubled over with laughter and absolutely of no use. The kitten continued to hiss. It was like fighting an alligator. I started to dissolve into giggles myself, but caught sight of someone approaching.

Martinez marched toward us, plucked the cat from Betty's head, then set the little thing on the ground. "We've made an arrest in the Thornton murder," he said without preamble. "Jack Bradley. We're holding a press conference at ten if you want to attend."

I blinked my eyes. "Jack Bradley? The environmental activist?"

"I demand you arrest these two," Betty ordered, doing her best to straighten her curls and failing. "They deliberately had that cat attack me."

Martinez ignored her. "His alibi fell apart. Security footage from Riverside Towers shows him leaving the building at 9 PM the night of the murder, not staying home as he claimed. And we found the murder weapon, the bloodied rock, hidden in his storage unit in the basement."

"I'm filing a complaint." Betty stormed away.

My heart sank. Jack Bradley. I'd seen him around the complex, passionate about saving green spaces, organizing petitions. He'd always seemed harmless if a bit intense. "You're sure it's him?"

"The evidence is solid. Rock matches the wound pattern on Thornton's skull. Blood on it is a match. Jack's fingerprints are on it. He claims it's because he picked it up from the park weeks ago to use as a doorstop, but that's a weak defense." Martinez paused. "I thought you'd want to know. You can finally relax. The threat is over." He gave a slight smile and meandered toward his squad car.

"Hmm." Lance frowned. "That's convenient."

"What do you mean?" I turned my attention to him.

"The murder weapon just sitting in his storage unit? Not destroyed, not thrown in a river, just... stored? After three weeks?" He shook his head. "That's either incredibly stupid or incredibly convenient for someone trying to frame him."

"Martinez seemed confident."

"Martinez has been under enormous pressure to solve this case. An arrest is an arrest, even if it's the wrong one." Lance shook his head. "I want to see that security footage. And I want to talk to Jack."

"Martinez said we could attend the press conference at ten."

"Not the press conference. Before that. I want to hear what Jack has to say before his lawyer tells him to stop talking."

We arrived at the police station at seven thirty, Lance using his temporary consultant credentials to get us past the front desk. Martinez was in his office, looking exhausted but satisfied.

"You're here early," he said, glancing up from paperwork.

"We want to talk to Jack Bradley," Lance said. "Before the press conference. Before this becomes official."

Martinez's eyes narrowed. "Why? We have our killer, Lance. Case closed."

"Humor me. Let us talk to him for five minutes. If I'm wrong, I'll apologize and buy you a beer. If I'm right, you'll thank me for catching it before you charged the wrong man."

After a long moment, Martinez nodded. "Five minutes. And I'm watching through the glass."

Jack Bradley sat in interrogation room two,

looking small and scared despite his tall frame. He was in his early forties, sandy-haired, with a receding hairline, wearing a wrinkled T-shirt that said "Save Our Parks." His hands were cuffed to the table.

"Mr. Bradley," Lance said as we entered. "I'm Lance Hendricks. This is Crystal Waters. We're not police, we're just trying to understand what happened."

Jack's eyes widened when he saw me. "You're the new owner of Riverside Towers. I've seen you around."

"That's right." I sat across from him, trying to appear non-threatening. "Jack, the police say you killed Richard Thornton. Did you?"

"No!" The word burst out of him. "I didn't kill anyone. I would never. I'm an activist, yes, but not a killer. I believe in legal protest, in changing hearts and minds, not violence."

"Then why did security footage show you leaving the building at 9 PM that night when you told police you were home all evening?" Lance asked.

Jack's shoulders slumped. "Because I was embarrassed. I wasn't home alone like I said. I was... meeting someone. Someone I shouldn't have been meeting."

"Who?" I asked gently.

"Emma Patterson." Jack's face flushed. "We've been seeing each other for a few months. She's married, separated, but technically still married. We're keeping it quiet until her divorce is final. That night, we met at her place. I left around nine, walked to her building, got there by nine fifteen, and stayed until almost midnight."

Lance and I exchanged glances. Emma Patterson. The dog walker who'd had an affair with Richard Thornton.

"Can Emma verify this?" Lance asked.

"She should, but..." Jack's voice dropped. "She's scared. Scared of her ex finding out, scared of being dragged into a murder investigation. When the police called her, she panicked and said she didn't know anything about that night."

"So, you have an alibi that your alibi won't confirm," I said.

"I know how it sounds. But I didn't kill Richard Thornton. Yeah, I hated what he was trying to do to the park. But I would never murder someone over it." Jack leaned forward as much as his cuffs allowed. "And that rock they found in my storage unit? I've never seen it before. Someone planted it there. Someone is framing me."

"Who has access to your storage unit?" Lance asked.

"It's in the basement of Riverside Towers. Any resident can access the basement. We all have the same key code for the door. Individual units have padlocks, but mine was broken last month. I kept meaning to replace it, but never got around to it." Jack's voice turned desperate. "Anyone could have put that rock there. Anyone at Riverside."

After we left the interrogation room, Martinez

waited in the hallway. "Well?"

"His alibi is Emma Patterson," Lance said. "Claims he was with her from nine fifteen to midnight that night."

"Emma Patterson denied knowing his whereabouts when we questioned her," Martinez countered.

"Because she's scared of her divorce being complicated." I looked at Martinez. "What if he's telling the truth? What if someone planted that rock in his storage unit because they knew his padlock was broken?"

Martinez rubbed his face. "Then we're back to square one with a killer who's smart enough to frame someone. But the evidence—"

"Is too convenient," Lance finished. "Murder weapon sitting in an accessible storage unit three weeks after the crime? That's not how criminals think. They panic, they destroy evidence, they hide it somewhere remote. They don't store it like a keepsake."

"Unless they're stupid," Martinez said.

"Jack Bradley isn't stupid. He's educated, organized enough to run successful protests. If he'd killed Thornton, he'd have been smarter about it." Lance crossed his arms. "Talk to Emma Patterson again. Push her on the alibi. If she verifies it, you have to release him."

"And if she doesn't?"

"Then maybe he is guilty. But at least you'll know

you checked every angle."

The press conference at ten was a media circus. Martinez announced Jack Bradley's arrest, detailed the evidence, and assured the public that the killer had been caught. Reporters shouted questions. Cameras flashed. The chief of police thanked Martinez for his diligent work.

I watched it all and felt sick to my stomach. What if Jack was innocent? What if the real killer was watching this, feeling safe now that someone else was taking the fall?

Back at Lance's apartment, I paced his living room while he made phone calls. Minnie followed me back and forth, sensing my anxiety.

"I want to test something," I said when Lance hung up. "When can we see Jack again?"

"Probably not until after he's arraigned. Why?"

"Minnie." I bent down to pet my little dachshund. "She's reacted to everyone connected to this case. She growled at Victoria Thornton. She was nervous around David Reeves when he came by. She even barked at Emma Patterson once. But I've seen her around Jack multiple times, and she's never reacted."

Lance stared at me. "Dogs can sense danger. Violence. Fear. If Jack had attacked Linda, had killed Thornton, Minnie might very well know."

"I know it sounds crazy—"

"It doesn't." Lance came over, taking my hands. "I've seen police dogs react to suspects before the handlers even identified them. Animals have instincts we've dulled in ourselves. If Minnie doesn't react to Jack, that's worth considering."

"What do we do? Martinez has his arrest. The press is celebrating. Everyone thinks it's over."

"We keep investigating. Privately." Lance's expression was determined. "Because I don't think Jack did it. The evidence is too neat, too convenient. Someone smart enough to avoid leaving fingerprints at the actual crime scene wouldn't be stupid enough to keep the murder weapon in an unsecured storage unit."

"Martinez told me to back off the investigation."

"He told you to back off. He didn't tell me." Lance smiled slightly. "And technically, I'm still consulting on this case. If I happen to investigate leads with my... girlfriend? Partner? Whatever we're calling this…that's just me doing my job."

My heart stuttered at the casual mention of labels. "Is that what I am? Your girlfriend?"

"I'd like you to be. If you want. Once we solve this murder, and no one's trying to kill you anymore." His thumb brushed across my knuckles. "I know the timing is terrible, and we're in the middle of chaos, but Crystal, working this case with you, protecting you, spending every day together, I haven't felt this alive since before Jake died."

"Lance—"

"Let me finish. For eight months, I've been going through the motions. Getting up, doing physical therapy, sitting at home, wondering if I'd ever be able to do my job again. Wondering if I even wanted to, knowing what I'd lost. But working with you, investigating together, protecting you has reminded me why I became a cop in the first place. To help people. To find justice. To make a difference."

His words made my eyes sting with tears. "I feel the same way. About working with you, about us. You make me feel safe even when I'm in danger. You make me feel capable even when I'm terrified. You—" I took a breath. "You make me feel like I'm not alone anymore."

He pulled me closer, his forehead resting against mine. "You're not alone. You'll never be alone as long as I'm breathing. And when this is over, when we catch whoever really killed Thornton, I want to explore what this is between us. Properly. With dates and dinners and no murder investigations hanging over our heads."

"I'd like that," I whispered.

"Good." He kissed me, soft and sweet and full of promise. When we pulled apart, his eyes were bright. "So. Should we keep investigating?"

"Absolutely." I felt renewed determination. "If Jack is innocent, we can't let him go to prison. And if the real killer is still out there, they're going to feel confident now. Cocky. They might make a mistake."

"That's what I'm counting on." Lance moved to his laptop, pulling up files. "Let's go through everything again. Every suspect, every piece of evidence, every contradiction. There's something we're missing. Something that will point us to the real killer."

We spent the rest of the day reviewing everything. Victoria's traffic camera footage and her claim that she found the body. David Reeves's embezzlement and his threat at the bar. Emma Patterson's affair and her matching jacket fabric. Mark Shuford being seen near the park. Linda's attack and her mysterious memory of seeing someone.

"It keeps coming back to Riverside Towers," I said, staring at our notes. "Everyone connected to this case has some connection to the property. Victoria wanted to develop it. David needed it for his business. Emma lives here. Mark's restaurant is nearby. Linda works and lives here. Jack lives here."

"And your aunt owned it." Lance looked up. "What if this isn't really about Richard Thornton at all? What if it's about the property?"

"But Aunt Mary Jane's death was ruled an accident. The medical records—"

"Could be legitimate. Or could be convenient." Lance's eyes narrowed. "What if someone killed your aunt to get control of the property, but you inherited instead of them? What if killing Thornton and framing various suspects has all been about clearing obstacles to get what they really want—Riverside Towers?"

A chill ran down my spine. "Then I'm not just a witness they need to silence. I'm the final obstacle."

"Which means we're running out of time." Lance

stood, determination written across his face. "We need to figure out who really killed Thornton before they come for you again. And this time, we need to be ready."

I looked down at Minnie, who was curled up at my feet, and thought about her reactions, or lack thereof, to Jack Bradley. Dogs knew things people didn't. They sensed danger, violence, and intent.

Whoever had killed Richard Thornton and attacked Linda Harper was still out there. Still dangerous. Still a threat.

But now Lance and I hunted them together, armed with suspicions and determination and the certainty that the wrong person had been arrested.

Jack Bradley might be behind bars, but the real killer was still free.

Not for long, though.

Not if we had anything to say about it.

"Let's catch a killer," I said.

Chapter Seventeen

Two days after Jack Bradley's arrest, I was going stir-crazy again. Lance had insisted I stay inside, stay safe, but the walls of his apartment, comfortable as they were, felt like they were closing in.

"One walk," I pleaded. "Just around the block. All three dogs need exercise, and I need fresh air and sunshine. Plus, you'll be with me. What could go wrong?"

Lance looked up from his laptop, where he'd been reviewing security footage from Riverside Towers for the hundredth time, looking for anything that might prove Jack's innocence. Dark circles shadowed his eyes from lack of sleep, and I felt a pang of guilt for adding to his stress.

"Fine," he finally said. "But we stay together. You don't leave my sight for even a second. And we bring King."

"Deal."

Twenty minutes later, we strolled down the sidewalk with four dogs on leashes, my three dachshunds trotting along happily and tangling around my legs, threatening to trip me on more than one occasion. King walked with military precision beside Lance. The afternoon was beautiful, warm but not hot, with that perfect spring weather that made everything feel possible.

"This is nice." The tension eased from my shoulders. "Just... normal. Like we're a regular couple taking our dogs for a walk."

"We are a regular couple." Lance took my hand in his. "We just happen to be investigating a murder and keeping you safe from a killer. But other than that, we're completely normal."

I laughed, and it felt good. We'd been so focused on the case, so consumed by danger and fear, that moments of levity had been rare. Walking beside him, our hands joined, dogs pulling us along, felt right.

We'd made it two blocks when I saw her.

Emma Patterson walked ahead of us on the sidewalk, pushing her dog walker cart—a modified jogging stroller designed to carry supplies while walking multiple dogs. She had four dogs with her today, all on leashes attached to her belt. She headed toward the park, probably for her afternoon walking route.

"There's Emma," I said quietly. "Should we—"
Minnie suddenly went crazy.

My sweet, timid, usually-anxious dachshund barked frantically and strained against her leash so hard I nearly dropped it. Not her usual nervous yapping, but deep, aggressive barks I'd never heard from her before. Her hackles were up, her entire body rigid with focus.

"Minnie, what—" I started.

But she'd already lunged forward with surprising strength, yanking the leash from my hand. She raced toward Emma Patterson, barking like she'd discovered her mortal enemy.

"Minnie!" I ran after her, heart pounding.

Emma turned at the sound. Her face went pale when she saw us. For just a second, our eyes met, and I saw something there—guilt? Fear? Panic?

Then I caught it. The scent. Expensive, floral, distinctive. The same perfume that had clung to the threatening note on my door, the same scent I'd noticed on the envelope when my apartment was ransacked.

"That perfume," I breathed.

Emma's eyes widened further, and she ran.

"Stop!" Lance shouted, already moving. He took off after Emma, King racing alongside him.

Emma dragged her dog walker cart behind her with four confused dogs still attached to her belt, the cart bouncing and rattling on the sidewalk. It slowed her down enough that Lance and King caught up quickly.

King positioned himself in front of the woman, not aggressive but immovable, his training making him a perfect barrier. Emma tried to dodge around him, but

Lance was already there, his hand on her arm.

"Emma Patterson, stop. We just want to talk."

"Get away from me!" She tried to twist free, her movement so violent that papers flew out of her cart, scattering across the sidewalk. Letters, documents, and photos all went tumbling in the breeze.

"Don't move," Lance commanded, and something in his voice, the cop voice, the voice of someone who'd spent years doing exactly this, made Emma freeze.

I caught up with Minnie, scooping her into my arms. She still growled, still focused on Emma with an intensity that made my skin crawl. I'd never seen my dog react to anyone like this. Ever.

While Lance kept hold of Emma, I bent to gather the scattered papers. The first thing I saw made my blood run cold.

A letter, handwritten, dated two months before Richard Thornton's murder.

David—

Richard is getting suspicious. The forensic accountant's appointment worries me. We need to move up our timeline. If he exposes the embezzlement before we can act, everything falls apart.

The affair story was a brilliant cover—now everyone thinks I'm a scorned lover with motive. But we both know this was never about Richard. It's about the property. Once he's gone and the widow sells, we can finally develop Riverside as planned.

Don't lose your nerve now. We've come too far.

*—E

My hands shook as I read it again. Emma and David. Working together. The affair with Richard had been a cover story, a way to establish a motive that would point away from the real plan.

"Lance," I said, my voice barely above a whisper. "Look at this."

He glanced at the letter while maintaining his grip on Emma. His features hardened. "Crystal, call Martinez. Now."

I fumbled for my phone while gathering more papers. More letters between Emma and David. Plans for developing Riverside Towers. Financial projections. A timeline that showed they'd been planning this for over a year.

And there, at the bottom of the pile, I found a receipt for the same expensive perfume I'd smelled. Dated the day before the first threatening note appeared.

"You." I narrowed my eyes at Emma. "You wrote the threatening notes. You broke into my apartment. You—"

"I didn't kill anyone!" Emma's voice was shrill. "That was all David. I just wanted the property deal to go through. I didn't sign up for murder."

"But you helped cover it up," Lance said. "You

created the affair story as motive. You planted evidence. You sent the threats to scare Crystal into selling."

Emma's face crumbled. "David said no one would get hurt. He said Richard would ruin everything, that we'd lose millions if the embezzlement was exposed. He said it would be quick, clean, an accident. But then Richard fought back, and there was blood everywhere, and—"

She cut herself off, realizing what she'd admitted.

Lance pulled out his phone with his free hand, calling Martinez while keeping Emma secured. His training was evident in every movement—the way he positioned himself, the calm in his voice despite the adrenaline that must be pumping through him, the professional assessment of the situation.

"Martinez, it's Hendricks. I've got Emma Patterson at the corner of Fifth and Maple. She's just confessed to conspiracy in the Thornton murder. David Reeves is your killer. I need units here now." He paused, listening. "Yes, I'm sure. Crystal found letters between Emma and David proving they planned it together. I'll secure the scene until you arrive."

People had stopped on the sidewalk, watching the drama unfold. Someone filmed on their phone. Emma's four client dogs barked in confusion and got tangled in their leashes.

I stood there holding my three dachshunds. Minnie still growled at Emma, Daisy and Bella pressed against my legs and watched Lance handle the situation with such confidence and competence that my chest ached.

This was who he was. Not a broken cop on medical leave, not someone lost and purposeless. This was Lance Hendricks doing what he was born to do—protecting people, finding truth, bringing justice.

And I'd been part of it. We'd done this together.

Martinez arrived with three patrol cars six minutes later. Officers took Emma into custody, carefully documenting the scattered papers that proved the conspiracy. Martinez listened to our statements, his expression growing darker with each detail.

"David Reeves?" he finally said. "You're sure?"

"The letters are explicit," Lance said. "Emma admits David killed Thornton. She claims she didn't know he was planning murder, just thought they were going to pressure Richard into backing off the forensic accountant. But she helped cover it up after, created the affair story as false motive, sent the threatening notes to Crystal."

"And Linda Harper?" I asked. "Did David attack her too?"

"Emma?" Martinez prompted.

Emma, now in handcuffs in the back of a patrol car, nodded. "David was afraid Linda had seen him that night at the park. When she started talking about remembering something, about dreams that might be memories, he panicked. He followed her to the park and attacked her before she could identify him."

"And Jack Bradley?" Lance asked. "The murder weapon in his storage unit?"

"David planted it. Jack's padlock was broken. Everyone knows that. David just walked in one night and hid the rock there, knowing it would be found eventually." Emma's voice was dull, defeated. "He thought it was brilliant. Frame the environmental activist, the one with obvious motive. No one would look deeper."

"Except we did," I said quietly.

Martinez organized a tactical team to arrest David Reeves. He'd fled to his lake house two hours outside the city, but had gone into hiding before they arrived.

Back at Lance's apartment, I collapsed on the couch with all three dogs piled on top of me. King lay at our feet, ever watchful. Lance sat beside me, his arm around my shoulders, both of us too exhausted to move.

"We did it," I said. "We've almost come to the end of who killed Thornton."

"You solved it," Lance corrected. "You noticed the perfume. You trusted Minnie's instincts. You gathered the evidence."

"You secured Emma. You called it in. You handled everything professionally." I turned to look at him.

We sat in comfortable silence for a while, processing everything that had happened. David Reeves had killed Richard Thornton to prevent the embezzlement from being exposed, knowing it would mean prison and financial ruin. Emma had helped plan it, thinking they'd just scare Richard into backing off, not realizing David intended murder.

They'd planted evidence to frame Jack Bradley. They'd sent threatening notes to scare me into selling Riverside Towers so they could proceed with their development plans. They'd attacked Linda to keep her quiet when she started remembering seeing David at the park that night.

And they'd failed because of a dog's instincts, an expensive perfume, and two people who refused to accept convenient answers.

Minnie chose that moment to worm her way between us, demanding attention. We laughed, and the tension broke, replaced by something lighter and warmer.

"She's a hero," Lance said, scratching Minnie's ears. "Knew Emma was dangerous before any of us did. We should get her a medal. Or at least a fancy new collar."

"She deserves both." I smiled down at my little dachshund, who'd been frightened and anxious through so much of this but had come through when it mattered most. "Good girl, Minnie. You caught a killer."

She licked my hand, then Lance's, then settled contentedly between us.

Outside, the sun was setting. Tomorrow, I'd have to deal with the aftermath. Statements to give, paperwork to sign, tenants to reassure. Tomorrow,

Lance would probably meet with the police psychologist about returning to active duty. And, the police would continue their search for Reeves.

Chapter Eighteen

After a day of high winds that left the parking lot full of leaves and other debris, I woke up determined to tackle property management duties. Emma Patterson was in custody, and David Reeves had fled. Life could return to normal—or as normal as life got when you'd survived a murder investigation and fallen for your handsome tenant-turned-boyfriend.

"I need to clean the parking lot," I told Lance over morning coffee. "The leaves are three inches deep in places, and I've already gotten two complaint emails."

Lance looked up from his laptop, where he reviewed reports for Martinez. "I'll come with you."

"You're busy. I'll be fine. The danger is over." I kissed his cheek, enjoying how natural the gesture had become. "Besides, you promised to walk King this morning. He's been giving you the stink eye for the past hour."

King, hearing his name, thumped his tail

hopefully.

"Fine," Lance said reluctantly. "But keep your phone on you. And take pepper spray. And—"

"And you installed that panic button app on my phone. I know. I'll be careful. It's just leaf blowing, not investigating murders." I smiled at his protective concern. "Go walk your dog. I'll be in the parking lot for maybe thirty minutes, then I'll come find you."

He didn't look entirely convinced, but he nodded. "Thirty minutes. Then I'm coming to check on you."

Since I couldn't keep an eye on my girls while using the loud leaf blower, I left Minnie, Daisy, and Bella in my apartment. They looked at me with betrayed expressions from the couch, but I couldn't risk them getting scared by the noise or running into the parking lot.

I put earbuds in to listen to a mystery audiobook, ironic, given what I'd just lived through, then unlocked the leaf blower from my storage shed and set off to clean the parking lot before more tenants complained. The morning was cool and clear, perfect weather for outdoor work.

The audiobook was a cozy mystery about a baker who solved murders, and I found myself critiquing the amateur detective's methods based on my recent experience. "That's not how you investigate a suspect," I muttered, even though no one could hear me over the leaf blower's roar.

As the tension in the book ramped up, I swept the

leaf blower back and forth faster and faster, caught up in the story. The speed at which I blew the leaves did nothing more than scatter them farther, rather than in a neat pile in the corner of the lot. I made more work for myself, but the physical activity felt good after days of being cooped up.

I'd made it halfway across the lot when I caught movement in my peripheral vision.

David Reeves stepped from behind a truck with a knife in his hand.

For one frozen second, my brain couldn't process what I saw. David Reeves. Who was supposed to be long gone from here. Who shouldn't be here, couldn't be here, except he was, and he had a knife, and—

I screamed and aimed the leaf blower at his face on pure instinct.

The powerful blast of air hit him directly, and he put up an arm to shield his face, stumbling backward. I didn't wait to see more. I threw the leaf blower at him. It clattered against his legs. Without another glance, I took off running across the parking lot.

How could I have let my guard down? How could I have been so stupid? I knew Reeves was dangerous, knew he'd killed Richard and attacked Linda. It should've been over.

Except clearly it wasn't.

My earbuds had fallen out during my sprint, and I could hear David behind me, his footsteps pounding on the pavement. I ducked behind a Suburban to catch my breath, my lungs burning, my heart hammering so hard I thought it might burst from my chest.

"You should have minded your own business, Ms. Waters." Reeves's voice was eerily calm, almost conversational. His feet crunched through leaves, getting closer. "Now, you've ruined my life. Someone has to pay for that, don't you think?"

No, I did not think I needed to pay for his crimes. He'd embezzled millions, murdered a man, attacked Linda, and terrorized me. This wasn't my fault—it was his.

Staying low, I crab-walked between cars, trying to put more distance between us. My knees scraped on the rough pavement, but I barely felt it. All I could think about was my backpack, sitting on the three-foot-high cement wall that separated the parking lot from the complex. My phone was in there.

If I could just reach it. If I could just trigger that button, Lance would come. Martinez would be alerted. Help would arrive.

But to reach the wall, I'd have to run into the open. Across at least twenty feet of exposed parking lot, where David would see me immediately.

Where were the tenants? By now, someone should've left their apartment to go somewhere. Mrs. Wilson usually went grocery shopping on Wednesday mornings. Betty Henderson walked to the community center for her book club. Someone should be here.

But the parking lot remained empty except for a

killer and me.

Despite the cool morning, perspiration ran down my back, soaking my shirt. I spotted my backpack, that familiar purple fabric like a beacon of hope. Twenty feet. I could run twenty feet. I'd done it at field day races in elementary school. I could do it now.

Except then I'd been running toward a finish line, not away from a man with a knife.

"If you come out now, Ms. Waters, I'll make this quick." Reeves sounded closer, forcing me to move again. I scrambled to the next car over, a minivan that provided better cover. "I can hear you scurrying like the little mouse you are. That makes me the mean Tom cat, wouldn't you say?"

The man was nuts. Completely, utterly insane. How had I not seen it before? How had any of us missed the instability behind his business-appropriate facade?

I glanced in the direction of the dog park. Lance had left to walk King almost an hour ago. He had to be returning soon, but would he get here in time to keep Reeves from killing me?

I had to get to that phone. Now.

Taking a deep breath, I burst from behind the minivan and ran. My legs pumped, arms swinging, everything focused on that purple backpack. Twenty feet became fifteen, became ten—

David appeared in front of me, somehow having circled around. He must have anticipated my move, must have been waiting. The knife gleamed in the morning sun.

I skidded to a stop, nearly falling, and changed direction. But he was faster. His hand shot out and grabbed my arm, yanking me backward with enough force that my feet left the ground.

"Gotcha," he hissed in my ear.

I struggled, kicking, scratching, doing everything I could to break free. My self-defense instincts kicked in—stomp on his instep, elbow to the ribs, make noise, attract attention. But his grip was iron-strong, and the knife was at my throat now, cold metal pressing against my skin.

"Stop fighting, or I'll cut you right here," he said.

I stopped, breathing hard, my mind racing. The panic button. If I couldn't reach my phone, I couldn't call for help. Lance wouldn't know I was in danger. Martinez wouldn't send backup.

I was alone.

Then I heard it. A sound I'd heard a thousand times before but had never been so grateful for. Barking. High-pitched, frantic, furious barking. Minnie.

My little dachshund, her sisters on her heels, came tearing across the parking lot like a tiny black and brown missile, her ears flying, her short legs pumping faster than I'd ever seen them move. Behind her, King ran with Lance who sprinted to keep up.

"Minnie, no!" I screamed, terrified David would hurt her.

But Minnie was fearless in a way I'd never seen before. She launched herself at David's ankle and bit down hard, her jaw locked with terrier determination.

David screamed and loosened his grip on me just enough. I threw myself forward, breaking free, and my hand closed around something in my pocket—the pepper spray Lance had insisted I carry. I spun and sprayed directly into David's face.

He howled, dropping the knife to claw at his eyes. Minnie released his ankle and darted behind me, still barking.

Lance got there in seconds, tackling David to the ground. They crashed into a car with a sickening thud, and Lance had David's arms pinned behind his back before I could even process what happened.

"Don't move," Lance commanded, and his cop voice was so authoritative that even I froze. King stood guard, his teeth bared, ready to intervene if needed.

Police sirens wailed in the distance, getting closer fast.

"How—" I gasped, trying to catch my breath. "How did you know?"

"I could see the two of you in the parking lot when I returned from walking King," Lance said, still holding David down. Tears from the pepper spray coursed down the man's face. He still tried to fight free, but Lance's knee was in his back, and he wasn't going anywhere. I called Martinez and ran."

"And Minnie?" I bent down to scoop up my brave

little dachshund, who trembled now that the adrenaline was wearing off.

"You must not have shut the door all the way." Lance's expression softened slightly as he looked at the dog. "She saved your life. That bite gave you the second you needed to break free."

Martinez arrived with three patrol cars. Officers swarmed the parking lot. They took over restraining David, who still cursed through his pepper-spray-induced tears.

I watched them load David into a patrol car, this time with charges that would ensure no bail—attempted murder, assault with a deadly weapon. He'd spend the rest of his life in prison.

It was over. Really, truly over.

My legs gave out, and Lance caught me, supporting my weight as the adrenaline crash hit. I shook so hard my teeth chattered.

"I've got you," he murmured, holding me close. "You're safe. You're okay."

"He was going to kill me."

"But he didn't. You fought back. You used the pepper spray. You kept your cool." Lance pulled back to look at me, his hands cupping my face. "You saved yourself, Crystal. You were so brave."

"I was terrified."

"Brave isn't the absence of fear. It's acting despite it." He kissed my forehead, gentle and reverent. "I'm so proud of you."

"And Minnie." I smiled at my little dachshund who now happily licked Lance's hand. "She's the real hero."

"She is," Lance agreed. "Best fifty pounds of guard dog I've ever seen."

"She weighs twelve pounds."

"Fifty pounds of courage in a twelve-pound body, then." He smiled, and despite everything, I smiled back.

Martinez approached with paperwork for me to sign. "Ms. Waters, I need a statement. But first, I need to apologize. I should have provided protection. This should never have happened."

"You caught him before he hurt me," I said. "Thanks to Lance and Minnie."

"Still. This was too close." Martinez looked at Lance. "Hendricks, the way you handled this—the panic button setup, the immediate response, the professional takedown—that's exactly what we need on the force. Have you thought about my offer to return to active duty?"

Lance was quiet for a moment, his arm still around me. "I have. And I think I'm ready. The injury is healed enough and today proved I can still do the job."

"Good. We'll start the paperwork." Martinez nodded at both of us. "You two make a hell of a team. Maybe we should hire you both."

"No, thanks." I gave a nervous giggle. "I'm going to stick to keeping my tenants happy."

After Martinez left to coordinate with his officers,

Lance and I sat on the cement wall, Minnie curled in my lap, Daisy and Bella perched beside me, and King sitting at our feet. The parking lot was still full of leaves, scattered even worse now from all the commotion. I'd have to start the cleanup all over again.

I leaned against Lance, exhausted and exhilarated and alive in a way I hadn't been in years. David Reeves was in custody. The case was closed. The danger was finally over.

And I had Lance—protective, capable, wonderful Lance—who'd become so much more than just my tenant or my boyfriend or even my partner in solving crimes.

He'd become my home.

"Thank you," I whispered.

"For what?"

"For everything. For protecting me, believing in me, loving me." I looked up at him. "You do love me, right? Because I love you, and it would be really awkward if—"

He kissed me, deep and thorough and full of promise. When we pulled apart, he was smiling.

"Yes, Crystal Waters. I love you. I think I have since I saw you covered in garbage disposal gunk, asking for help."

"That's ridiculous. I wasn't covered—"

"You were definitely covered."

"Fine. But I love you too. Since you smiled at me for the first time and I realized how handsome you are when you're not brooding."

"I don't brood."

"You absolutely brood."

We dissolved into laughter, the tension and fear finally breaking. Around us, police officers were finishing their investigation. Tenants had started emerging from their apartments, curious about the commotion. Life at Riverside Towers was returning to normal.

But for Lance and me, nothing would ever be normal again.

We'd caught a killer together. We'd fallen in love. We'd both discovered who we were meant to be.

And we'd done it all with three tiny dachshunds and one very patient German Shepherd by our sides.

"Come on." Lance stood and pulled me up with him. "Let's go home. You need rest, and these leaves can wait for another day."

"Home," I repeated, liking how that sounded. "Your apartment or mine?"

"Either one," he said. "Wherever we're together, that's home."

And holding his hand, surrounded by dogs and debris and the aftermath of danger survived, I knew he was right.

Chapter Nineteen

Three days after David Reeves tried to kill me in the parking lot, Lance and I sat in Martinez's office listening to the full confession recordings. Martinez had wanted us to hear them; said we'd earned the right to know exactly what had happened and why.

"This is David Reeves' confession." Martinez pressed play on the first recording.

David's voice filled the room, arrogant even in defeat. "Of course, I planned it. I'm not an idiot. Richard was going to expose the embezzlement, ruin everything I'd built. I couldn't let that happen."

"Tell me about the night of the murder," Martinez's recorded voice prompted.

"I'd been planning it for weeks, but Emma kept losing her nerve. Said we should just pay back the money, come clean. She didn't understand that there was no coming clean from $2 million in embezzlement. That's prison time, lost everything time." David's tone was bitter. "So, I told her we'd just scare Richard, make him back off the forensic accountant. Get him to agree to a payment plan, something we could manage."

"But that's not what you did."

"No. I went to the park that night with the intention of killing him. I'd asked him to meet me there, saying I wanted to discuss the embezzlement privately, away from offices and lawyers. He agreed because he was naive enough to think I'd cooperate." A laugh, cold and hollow. "I brought a rock from my garden, wrapped in a towel. Thought I'd make it look like a mugging gone wrong."

Lance tensed beside me, his hand finding mine under the table. My stomach dropped as the recording continued.

"What happened?" Martinez prompted.

"Richard showed up right on time and started lecturing me about integrity and consequences. Like he was so perfect, so above reproach. I lost my temper. Told him I'd worked too hard to let him destroy me. That's when he said he'd already sent copies of the forensic accountant's preliminary findings to the board of directors. That it was too late to stop it."

David paused, and I could hear him breathing heavily on the recording.

"I hit him. Once, hard, on the back of the head. He went down like a stone. I stood there for a minute, watching him bleed, thinking maybe I could still fix this. But then Emma showed up."

Martinez stopped the recording. "This is where Emma's version differs significantly. Let me play hers."

My grip tightened on Lance's.

Emma's voice was smaller, frightened. "David said we were just going to talk to Richard. Convince him to give us more time. I swear, that's what I thought we were doing."

"But you brought a weapon," Martinez's voice said.

"A rock. I found it near the park entrance. David said we might need to defend ourselves if Richard got violent. He'd been so angry lately, making threats. I was scared." Emma's voice cracked. "When I got there, David and Richard were arguing. Richard turned to leave and said he was calling the police. That's when I panicked."

My stomach twisted.

"I didn't mean to hit him so hard. I just wanted him to stop…to listen. But the rock…I hit him on the temple, and he just... collapsed. There was so much blood." Emma sobbed now on the recording. "David said we had to finish it, that we couldn't let him survive to identify us. He took the rock from me and hit Richard again. And again."

Martinez stopped that recording, too. "So, they both claim to have struck Richard, but both blame the other for the fatal blows. Forensics confirms multiple impacts—the medical examiner found three distinct strike patterns. David's story has him hitting Richard once. Emma has her hitting once, and David finishing it. The truth is probably somewhere in between."

"They both killed him," Lance said flatly.

"Yes. Legally, they're both culpable for murder regardless of who struck which blow. Joint enterprise, acting in concert." Martinez pulled out another file. "But there's more. The frame-up of Jack Bradley was elaborate."

He played another segment of David's confession.

"Jack was perfect—an environmental activist with a clear motive, a storage unit with a broken padlock that everyone knew about. Emma planted the rock there three days after the murder. We'd kept it wrapped in plastic, preserved the blood evidence. Made it look like he'd been too stupid to dispose of it properly."

"And the letters? The evidence in his unit?" Martinez asked.

"Those were Emma's idea. She wrote threatening letters in disguised handwriting, planted them in Jack's apartment when she was 'dog sitting' for a neighbor on his floor. We knew the police would search his place once they found the weapon. We wanted to make sure they found enough evidence to convict."

I shook my head, disgusted. "They were going to let an innocent man go to prison."

"They almost succeeded," Martinez said grimly. He played more of Emma's confession.

"The night Linda Harper was attacked, well, that was a mistake. David thought he saw Victoria Thornton returning to the park. He'd been watching the area, paranoid that she'd seen something the night of the murder. When he saw a woman with dark hair walking dogs early in the morning, he assumed it was Victoria coming back to the scene."

"But it was Linda Harper," Martinez's voice confirmed.

"Yes. David realized it too late. Linda fought back, tried to scream. He beat her to keep her quiet, then fled when he heard someone approaching. He told me later that he'd left her for dead." Emma's voice was hollow with horror. "I didn't know he was going to hurt anyone else. I swear I didn't know."

Martinez stopped the recording and looked at me. "She claims ignorance, but the evidence tells a different story. Emma sent all the threatening notes to you. She ransacked your apartment while David kept watch. She helped plan every step of the cover-up."

"She's as guilty as he is," Lance said.

"Agreed. Both are being charged with first-degree murder, conspiracy, assault with intent to kill, witness tampering, and about a dozen other charges. Neither is getting out of prison in this lifetime." Martinez pulled out one more document. "There's one more thing. The buried wallet with $5,000 and that threatening letter? Complete red herring."

"What?" I leaned forward.

"Richard Thornton was being blackmailed by someone completely unrelated to this case. A former business partner who knew about some shady dealings from years ago. Richard buried the cash and letter, intending to use them as evidence against the blackmailer if needed. David and Emma didn't even know about it. They were as surprised as we were when Minnie dug it up."

I sat back, processing this. "So that whole piece of evidence had nothing to do with his murder?"

"Nothing. Just unfortunate timing that made our investigation more complicated." Martinez smiled slightly. "Though it did lead us to take a closer look at Richard's finances, which helped confirm David's embezzlement. So, it wasn't entirely useless."

Lance shook his head. "A murder investigation with dueling confessions, a frame-up, mistaken identity, and a blackmail red herring. This case had everything."

"Except for an easy solution," Martinez agreed. He turned to Lance. "Which brings me to why I asked you both here. Hendricks, your work on this case was exceptional. The way you saw through the frame-up, caught the inconsistencies, protected Ms. Waters— that's exactly what we need on the force."

"I'm on medical leave—" Lance started.

"I know. And I know you're worried about passing the physical fitness requirements." Martinez held up a hand. "But I'm offering you a consulting position. Desk work, case analysis, and training new detectives. You'd still be doing the job you love, just from a different angle. The injury wouldn't be a factor.

This is only until you're released for active duty, then I want you on the force."

Lance sat quietly, his expression thoughtful. I squeezed his hand under the table, letting him know I supported whatever he decided.

"Can I think about it?" Lance finally asked.

"Of course. Take your time. But Hendricks, you're one of the best detectives I've ever worked with. It would be a shame to lose you because of a physical limitation that doesn't limit your abilities where they matter most." Martinez stood, extending his hand. "Think about it and let me know."

After we left Martinez's office, Lance and I strolled to a nearby coffee shop. We ordered our usual, black coffee for him, vanilla latte for me, and sat at a table by the window.

"A consulting position," I said. "That's perfect, isn't it? You could still do the work you love without worrying about the physical requirements."

"It's not the same, though. I'd be behind a desk while other detectives do the fieldwork." Lance stared into his coffee. "Part of me wants to say yes immediately. But another part feels like I'd be giving up, accepting that I can't do the job properly anymore."

"That's not what it is. You heard Martinez. This is only temporary." I reached across the table for his hand. "You solved this case, Lance. You, with your instincts, experience, and brilliant mind. You didn't need to chase suspects or kick down doors to do that. You just needed to be yourself."

"But I like chasing suspects and kicking down doors," he said with a slight smile.

"I know. But would you rather give up detective work entirely or adapt it to something you can still do?" I paused. "And it wouldn't be forever, necessarily. Maybe in a few months, a year, your knee heals enough to pass the physical. Then you could go back to fieldwork. But in the meantime, you'd still be helping people. Still making a difference."

He was quiet for a long moment, then smiled. "When did you get so wise?"

"I learned from this very patient, very capable detective who taught me that being brave means acting despite fear, and being smart means knowing when to adapt." I smiled back. "Sound familiar?"

"Vaguely." He lifted my hand to his lips, kissing my knuckles. "You're right. I'll call Martinez tomorrow and accept the position. It's not giving up—it's evolving."

"Exactly." I felt relief wash through me. Lance returning to work, even in a consulting role, meant he'd have purpose again. Direction. The confidence that came from using his skills to help people.

"What about you?" Lance asked. "Have you decided what you want to do? Property management or something else?"

I'd been thinking about this constantly since the attack in the parking lot. "I want to keep Riverside

Towers. It was Aunt Mary Jane's legacy, and I feel connected to it now. In my spare time, I'm going to volunteer with a search and rescue dog organization, see if Minnie or one of the puppies has the aptitude for it." Excitement built. "I want to help people the way we helped solve this case. I want to use what I learned, what I'm good at."

Lance's eyes lit up. "That's perfect."

We sat there smiling at each other like idiots, and I didn't care who saw us. Three weeks ago, I'd been a directionless property manager who'd never solved anything more complicated than a stopped-up toilet.

"What about us?" Lance asked. "We've been living in my apartment since the threats started. Do we keep doing that? Do you want your own space back?"

"Honestly? I like living with you. Your apartment feels more like home than mine ever did." I hesitated. "But, I'd really like to stay in my own place for a while."

"Of course. I love you, Crystal. I want whatever makes you happy."

"Thank you." The words came out without hesitation. "I love you too." Things had moved so fast over the last few weeks that my head spun. I needed time to sort it all out.

We walked back to Riverside Towers in comfortable silence, our hands joined, our future stretching ahead of us bright with possibility. David and Emma would spend the rest of their lives in prison. Jack

Bradley had been cleared and released with profuse apologies. Linda Harper was recovering well.

Aunt Mary Jane would have been proud. She'd left me her property hoping I'd find my way, find myself, find something worth fighting for.

I'd found all of that and more.

"Hey," Lance said as we reached my apartment. "Thank you."

"For what?"

"For knocking on my door covered in garbage disposal gunk. For being brave and stubborn and refusing to give up. For reminding me who I am and what I'm capable of." He cupped my face in his hands. "For loving me when I was too broken to see I was worth loving."

"You were never broken. Just hurt. There's a difference." I stood on my toes to kiss him. "And you did the same for me. Showed me I was capable of more than I thought. Made me brave when I was terrified. Loved me when I was just a mess of a property manager who couldn't fix a toilet."

"You can fix toilets now."

"Barely." I laughed.

We kissed and went inside to where three dachshunds and one German Shepherd were waiting, tails wagging, ready for dinner and walks and all the normal, beautiful, non-murder-related parts of life.

The case was closed. The killers were caught.

Justice had been served.

    The end of one chapter.

    The beginning of another.

    And I couldn't wait to see what came next.

Epilogue

Six weeks after David and Emma's arrest, life had settled into a new rhythm. My days were spent handling the day-to-day operations of Riverside Towers. Lance had accepted Martinez's consulting position and spent his days at the police station, analyzing cold cases and mentoring new detectives. Our evenings were spent together—cooking dinner, walking the dogs, planning our future.

But we still hadn't been on a proper date.

"The dog park?" I suggested when Lance came home from work looking restless. "The weather's perfect."

"Yeah. Let's go."

We gathered all four dogs, my three dachshunds and King, and walked the familiar three blocks. The late afternoon sun cast everything in golden light, and the air had that perfect spring warmth that made you want to be outside forever.

The park was mostly empty at this hour, just a few dedicated dog owners throwing balls and chatting. Lance and I claimed our usual bench while the dogs ran and played. Minnie had come so far from the anxious, trembling pup she'd been. She chased after Daisy and Bella with confidence, even playing with King without fear.

"She's like a different dog," I said, watching Minnie race across the grass.

"She learned she was braver than she thought." Lance's shoulder pressed against mine, warm and solid. "Kind of like her owner."

I smiled. "I had a good teacher."

"You were always brave. You just didn't know it yet."

We sat in comfortable silence for a few minutes, watching the sunset paint the sky in oranges and pinks. This park had been the site of so much darkness—Richard's murder, our investigation, moments of fear and danger. But it was also where I'd met Lance. Where Minnie had found the wallet that broke the case open. Where we'd become partners.

"Crystal," Lance said, and something in his tone made me turn to look at him. "I need to ask you something."

My heart rate picked up. "Okay."

"Would you like to go to dinner with me? Tomorrow night. A real date, not just discussing cases over coffee or eating takeout on the couch. Somewhere nice, where I can take you out properly and show you that I know how to be romantic when I'm not chasing killers or analyzing evidence."

My smile grew impossibly wide. "Lance Hendricks, are you asking me on a date?"

"I'm trying to. I'm a bit out of practice." He rubbed the back of his neck, looking adorably uncertain. "Is that a yes?"

"Yes. Absolutely yes." I laughed. "I was beginning to think you'd forgotten we were supposed to do the normal dating thing."

"I didn't forget. I just wanted to wait until things were settled. Until we had breathing room to be normal." He took my hand, threading our fingers together. "You deserve romance, Crystal. Candlelight, good wine, and conversation that isn't about murder. You deserve to be courted."

"Courted?" I teased. "What century are you from?"

"The century where I want to do this right." His dark eyes held mine, serious and intense. "I want to take you on dates. I want to bring you flowers and open doors for you and make you feel special."

"I already feel special." I squeezed his hand. "But I'd love to go to dinner with you. And yes to the flowers and door-opening and all of it."

Relief flooded his face. "Good. Because I already made reservations at that Italian place downtown. Seven o'clock tomorrow. And I bought you flowers.

They're in my truck."

"You already bought flowers?" I laughed. "What if I'd said no?"

"Then I'd have tried again. And again. Until you said yes." He smiled, and it transformed his face from handsome to devastating. "I'm persistent when I want something. And I want you, Crystal Waters. For dates, adventures, and solving mysteries together. For lazy Sunday mornings and midnight conversations. For everything."

My breath caught. "Lance—"

"I know it's fast. I know we've only been together a couple months. But when you've faced death together, when you've trusted someone with your life and your heart, you know." He cupped my face with his free hand. "I know this is real. I know you're it for me. And I'm not waiting to tell you."

"You're it for me too," I whispered. "You walked into my life when I needed you most—when I didn't even know I needed you. You made me brave. You made me believe I could be more than I was. You—"

He kissed me.

Not the quick kisses we'd shared before, not the gentle pecks or hurried touches while rushing to investigate. This was different. This was deliberate, thorough, and full of promise. His hand slid into my hair, the other still holding mine, and I melted into him.

When we finally pulled apart, the sun had dipped lower, painting everything in deep gold and crimson.

Around us, the other dog owners had discreetly moved away, giving us privacy.

"Wow," I breathed.

"Yeah." Lance rested his forehead against mine. "I've wanted to do that properly for weeks."

"You should have done it sooner."

"I'll make up for lost time." He kissed me again, softer this time, sweeter.

Minnie barked, demanding attention, and we broke apart laughing. Our four dogs had gathered at our feet, tails wagging, as if they approved of this development.

"I should tell you something," Lance said, still holding me close. "I moved to Riverside Towers to hide. After Jake died, after the injury, I couldn't face the world. Couldn't face myself. I just wanted somewhere quiet where I could disappear, and no one would expect anything from me."

"And then I knocked on your door covered in garbage disposal gunk."

"And then you asked me for help." He smiled. "And suddenly I had a reason to get up in the morning. A murder to solve, a woman to protect, a purpose again. You and this case—you reminded me why I became a detective. To protect people. To seek justice. To make a difference."

"You made a difference to me," I said. "You still do. Every day."

"Good. Because I plan to keep making a

difference to you for a very long time." He stood, pulling me up with him. We gathered our dogs and started the walk back to Riverside Towers, hand in hand. The sunset had given way to twilight, and the first stars were appearing overhead.

We stood there in the doorway of Riverside Towers. The place where it all began, where a broken cop and a lost property manager had found each other in the midst of murder and mayhem. Where three dachshunds and a German Shepherd had become heroes. Where justice had been served, and love had bloomed in the most unexpected way.

Tomorrow we'd have our first real date. Tomorrow we'd start the next chapter.

But tonight, standing under the stars with the man I loved and our four dogs at our feet, I knew I was exactly where I was supposed to be.

THE END

www.cynthiahickey.com
Cynthia Hickey is a multi-published and best-selling author of cozy mysteries and romantic suspense/thrillers. She has taught writing at many conferences and small writing retreats. She and her husband run the publishing press, Winged Publications. They live in Arizona and Arkansas, becoming snowbirds with three dogs. They have ten grandchildren who keep them busy and tell everyone they know that "Nana is a writer."

Connect with me on FaceBook
Twitter
Sign up for my newsletter and receive a free short story
www.cynthiahickey.com

Follow me on Amazon
And Bookbub
Shop my bookstore on my website for better prices and autographed books.

Enjoy other books by Cynthia Hickey

Romantic Suspense and Thrillers

The Sheriff of Misty Hollow
Girls' Weekend Survival
The Threat
Evil Returns
Drowned in Silence
Banner of Death
Christmas Burns
High Stakes

Cowboys of Misty Hollow
Cowboy Jeopardy
Cowboy Peril
Cowboy Hazard
Cowgirl Blaze
Cowboy Uncertainty
Cowboy Christmas Crisis
Cowboy Pitfall
Snowed in For Christmas With a Cowboy

Stay on the Ranch with the whole set

Misty Hollow
Secrets of Misty Hollow
Deceptive Peace
Calm Surface

Lightning Never Strikes Twice
Lethal Inheritance
Bitter Isolation
Say I Don't
Christmas Stalker
Bridge to Safety
When Night Falls
A Place to Hide
Mountain Refuge

Stay in Misty Hollow for a while. Get the entire series here!

Secrets of the South
The Lovers' Lane Murders
The Prom Night Hitchhiker
Up in Smoke

The Seven Deadly Sins series
Deadly Pride
Deadly Covet
Deadly Lust
Deadly Glutton
Deadly Envy
Deadly Sloth
Deadly Anger
Get the whole set here

Brothers Steele
<u>Sharp as Steele</u>
<u>Carved in Steele</u>
<u>Forged in Steele</u>
<u>Brothers Steele</u> (All three in one)

The Brothers of Copper Pass
<u>Wyatt's Warrant</u>
<u>Dirk's Defense</u>
<u>Stetson's Secret</u>
<u>Houston's Hope</u>
<u>Dallas's Dare</u>
<u>Seth's Sacrifice</u>
<u>Malcolm's Misunderstanding</u>
<u>The Brothers of Copper Pass Boxed Set</u>

Highland Springs

<u>Murder Live</u>
<u>Say Bye to Mommy</u>
<u>To Breathe Again</u>
<u>Highland Springs Murders</u> (all 3 in one)

Colors of Evil Series

<u>Shades of Crimson</u>

Coral Shadows
Indigo Nightmares
Read the whole set!

The Pretty Must Die Series

Ripped in Red, book 1
Pierced in Pink, book 2
Wounded in White, book 3
Worthy, The Complete Story

Lisa Paxton Mystery Series

Eenie Meenie Miny Mo
Jack Be Nimble
Hickory Dickory Dock
Boxed Set

Hearts of Courage
A Heart of Valor
The Game
Suspicious Minds
After the Storm
Local Betrayal
Hearts of Courage Boxed Set

Overcoming Evil series

<u>Mistaken Assassin</u>
<u>Captured Innocence</u>
<u>Mountain of Fear</u>
<u>Exposure at Sea</u>
<u>A Secret to Die for</u>
<u>Collision Course</u>
<u>Romantic Suspense of 5 books in 1</u>

Wife for Hire – Private Investigators
<u>Saving Sarah</u>
<u>Lesson for Lacey</u>
<u>Mission for Meghan</u>
<u>Long Way for Lainie</u>
<u>Aimed at Amy</u>
<u>Wife for Hire</u> (all five in one)

<u>One Hour (A short story thriller)</u>
<u>One Night (a short story thriller)</u>
<u>One Day</u>
<u>One (the set)</u>

COZY MYSTERIES

The Tail Waggin' Mysteries
<u>Cat-Eyed Witness</u>
<u>The Dog Who Found a Body</u>

<u>Troublesome Twosome</u>
<u>Four-Legged Suspect</u>
<u>Unwanted Christmas Guest</u>
<u>Wedding Day Cat Burglar</u>
<u>The entire Tail Waggin' Series</u>

Tiny House Mysteries
<u>No Small Caper</u>
<u>Caper Goes Missing</u>
<u>Caper Finds a Clue</u>
<u>Caper's Dark Adventure</u>
<u>A Strange Game for Caper</u>
<u>Caper Steals Christmas</u>
<u>Caper Finds a Treasure</u>
<u>Tiny House Mysteries boxed set</u>

A Hollywood Murder
<u>Killer Pose, book 1</u>
<u>Killer Snapshot, book 2</u>
<u>Shoot to Kill, book 3</u>
<u>Kodak Kill Shot, book 4</u>
<u>To Snap a Killer</u>
<u>Hollywood Murder Mysteries</u>

Shady Acres Mysteries

<u>Beware the Orchids</u>
<u>Path to Nowhere</u>
<u>Poison Foliage</u>
<u>Poinsettia Madness</u>
<u>Deadly Greenhouse Gases</u>
<u>Vine Entrapment</u>
<u>Shady Acres Boxed Set</u>

Nosy Neighbor Series
<u>Anything For A Mystery</u>
<u>A Killer Plot</u>
<u>Skin Care Can Be Murder</u>
<u>Death By Baking</u>
<u>Jogging Is Bad For Your Health</u>
<u>Poison Bubbles</u>
<u>A Good Party Can Kill You</u>
<u>Nosy Neighbor collection</u>

<u>Christmas with Stormi Nelson</u>

The Summer Meadows Series
<u>Fudge-Laced Felonies</u>
<u>Candy-Coated Secrets</u>
<u>Chocolate-Covered Crime</u>
<u>Maui Macadamia Madness</u>
<u>All four novels in one collection</u>

The River Valley Mystery Series
<u>Deadly Neighbors</u>
<u>Advance Notice</u>
<u>The Librarian's Last Chapter</u>
<u>All three novels in one collection</u>

Cozies not part of a series
<u>Coffee, Tea, or Murder</u>
<u>Scones to Die For</u>
<u>Mischief and Mayhem</u>

Time Travel
<u>The Portal</u>

Historical cozy
<u>Hazel's Quest</u>

Historical Romances
Novellas
<u>Runaway Sue</u>
<u>Taming the Sheriff</u>
<u>Sweet Apple Blossom</u>
<u>A Doctor's Agreement</u>
<u>A Lady Maid's Honor</u>
<u>A Touch of Sugar</u>

Love Over Par
Heart of the Emerald
A Sketch of Gold
Her Lonely Heart
Abigail's Proposal
Sophia's Hope
Moira's Quest
Savannah's Trial
Josephine's Dream
A Most Reluctant Bride
Competing Hearts
A Teacher's Heart
Lesson of Love

SERIES
Finding Love the Harvey Girl Way
Cooking With Love
Guiding With Love
Serving With Love
Warring With Love
All 4 in 1

Finding Love in Disaster
The Rancher's Dilemma
The Teacher's Rescue

<u>The Soldier's Redemption</u>

Woman of courage Series

<u>A Love For Delicious</u>
<u>Ruth's Redemption</u>
<u>Charity's Gold Rush</u>
<u>Mountain Redemption</u>
<u>They Call Her Mrs. Sheriff</u>
<u>Woman of Courage series</u>

Short Story Westerns
<u>Flowers of the Desert</u>

Contemporary

Romance in Paradise
<u>Maui Magic</u>
<u>Sunset Kisses</u>
<u>Deep Sea Love</u>
<u>3 in 1</u>

The Red Hat's Club (Contemporary novellas)

<u>Finally</u>
<u>Suddenly</u>
<u>Surprisingly</u>

The Red Hat's Club 3 – in 1

STANDALONES
Finding a Way Home
Service of Love
Hillbilly Cinderella
Unraveling Love
I'd Rather Kiss My Horse

Whisper Sweet Nothings (a Valentine short romance)

Christmas Romances (Contemporary and Historical)
Dear Jillian
Romancing the Fabulous Cooper Brothers
Handcarved Christmas
The Payback Bride
Curtain Calls and Christmas Wishes
Christmas Gold
A Christmas Stamp
Snowflake Kisses
Merry's Secret Santa
Holly's Hope
A Christmas Deception
A Christmas Castle

Heads up! Some of the links above are affiliate links. If you decide to buy through them, I may earn a small commission (thank you for supporting my work!). It doesn't change the price for you.

www.ingramcontent.com/pod-product-compliance
Lightning Source LLC
Chambersburg PA
CBHW060303310726
48976CB00007B/2192